Blood on
the Snow

Pamela Lamb

Agneau Press
2009

First published 2009 by Agneau Press,
Email: agneaupress@optusnet.com.au

ISBN 978-0-9580489-4-1

Cover image from an original photograph by
Christa Belle Harrison (www.christabelle.com)

Pamela Lamb grew up on the Wirral in the north of England. She migrated to Australia in 1969 and has lived in Ipswich since 1974, so she is almost a local. She has three children and two grandchildren, and lives happily with her old bull terrier, Bob, and the birds in the garden. Pamela had been writing for 15 years, mostly for children and young adults.

ONE

'Who the fuck are you?'

It had taken all my strength to raise my eye lids half-way but still the light was painful. White ceiling. White walls. Cold air, scrubbed clean. The quiet hum of machinery. I knew without being told that I was underground. Under the covers of the bed my left leg screamed in an agony so intense it threatened to black me out again.

The face was that of a black man. A big black man in a white coat. At the sound of my voice his face split into a wide grin.

'I'm Nurse James Nixon, ma'am, and I'm might pleased to see you're awake at last. Now just you hang on here and I'll go and git the doc.'

I watched him walk silently along the low-ceilinged room towards a door at the far end. They'd given me a drug. I could feel it in my brain like cotton wool. It was hard to think. But at least I knew where I was. Amundsen base. It had to be. There wasn't anywhere else in Antarctica that would have a hospital this size.

'Zoe Carter?'

Another man stood by the bed. Small. White. Middle-aged. I nodded my head. Stopped quickly. There was pain there, too, that the drug disguised.

'I'm Jason Kennedy. How are you feeling?'

'I feel like shit.'

Warm, smooth doctor's hands gripped my wrist.

'That's understandable. You're lucky to be alive. Do you remember what happened?'

A flash of pain. 'I crashed my 'copter. Is Colin okay?'

I saw the doctor's gaze flick up to the face of the big black nurse and the answering shake of his head. I felt panic rise in my throat.

'But he must be here. He was in the helicopter. With me.'

'I'm sorry, Miss Carter. I guess they'll try and retrieve his body when the weather lifts. It's blowing one hell of a gale right now.'

His body?

I had the urge to lift myself onto one elbow and yell, 'Go out and get him *now*,' but my body refused to cooperate. Besides, I knew quite well that, even if Colin had survived the crash, there's no way he'd still be alive now. Not out there.

The doctor lifted my wrist to take my pulse. 'You're with Brightsward, aren't you? Off that boat they've got parked down in McMurdo Sound.'

I could hear the disdain, thinly veiled, that all Antarctic residents felt towards the summer cowboys. And, oh yeah, he really did it tough, didn't he? Down here in his centrally heated dome with slabs of steak in the freezer and fresh orange juice for breakfast.

'The *Astral Traveller*,' I said, careful to remember not to nod my head.

Through the drug-induced fog, my mind presented me with a tiny, crystal-clear image of the old ice breaker as I'd lifted my helicopter from her deck. The trail of black smoke from the funnel, the flick, flick of the radar on its white pole and, below my feet, the bullseye target of the landing pad where I was going to touch down as light as a butterfly, showing off my flying skills to the attractive young man sitting in the passenger seat, his thigh warm against mine. And, as I'd climbed higher and banked my craft to head towards land, there on the ship's rusty flank was the environmental group's rainbow-coloured logo obscured, after three months in the Southern Ocean, by a thick layer of salt and grime.

Dr Kennedy nodded, unrestrained by the agony that resided inside my skull. 'We've been in touch with your people. They're going to have you out of here in no time.' I felt a slim needle penetrate my arm. 'Now, get yourself some rest.' He gripped my hand, smiled with his teeth and withdrew his head from my field of vision.

My sister Zara was waiting for me on the platform. The air was humid, perfumed with frangipani and the sharp scent of flying ants. Thick grey clouds were draped across the tops of the low hills. She took a step forward.

'Can I help?'

'No, it's okay. I can manage.'

I threw my backpack onto the platform and climbed down awkwardly from the train.

'How are you, Zoe? I wasn't expecting the stick.'

'It's not permanent. Where are the kids?'

'Tina's in school. I left Lisa playing in next-door's pool. It's too hot to drag kids around.'

'You're not wrong about the heat.'

Released from the air-conditioned train, my leg set up an insistent, throbbing ache. I had painkillers in my pack but they'd have to wait until I was by myself. I didn't want to give my sister another reason to mother me. Zara picked up my backpack and led the way to the car park, walking slowly to accommodate my limp and drive me mad.

'Your things arrived yesterday. From Argentina.' Her eyes opened wide. 'What were you doing in Argentina?' For a Bowen girl, born and bred, it might as well have been the moon.

'I was in hospital. Getting my leg fixed. What things?'

'Personal possessions, it said on the box. Clothes, CDs, books.'

'Everything, then.'

'If that's all you've got.'

Zara had a brand new house, a kitchen full of gadgets and a late model car. And wanted more.

'All that stuff was in my cabin on the *Astral Traveller*. I wonder why they've sent it here?'

'Oh, Zoe, you're not thinking of going back there, are you? Not after what happened.'

'I don't know what else I'm going to do.'

What I did was lower myself gratefully onto the cool sheets

of my sister's spare bed, swallow my painkillers with a mug of lukewarm tea and watch the ceiling fan turn slowly until the blackness came.

Later, in that half state between waking and sleeping, I heard my niece come home from school, smelled the scent of rain-soaked earth as the afternoon storm passed over and, finally, opened my eyes to the sight of my brother-in-law, Derek Antonino, standing in the doorway.

'How's the patient?' He came forward into the room. 'Zara says you're in a bit of pain.'

I had hated my sister's husband since the day I first clapped eyes on him and he hated me in return. It was a guilty secret we kept from Zara.

'No, no, I'm fine.' I struggled to sit up and he watched. 'When's dinner?'

'Not long. Zara's just feeding the girls. D'you want a hand?'

'I wouldn't mind a drink.'

It was Wednesday night and they never drank mid-week. It was one of Derek's rules which I knew he broke because I'd seen the whisky bottle in the shed where he kept his computer and his dirty magazines.

He lifted his lip over his teeth. 'I've brought home a bottle of wine. As a bit of a celebration.'

Plonk would have been a better word for it. It took two lumps of ice to make it bearable.

'Well, here's cheers, girls.'

Over the rim of the glass I watched him watching me and wondered how long I could stand it this time.

The next morning Zara took me to see our mother. The nursing home was out of town along the highway going north. I waited until she'd negotiated the busy traffic in town and was accelerating onto the straight strip of bitumen. Then I said, 'How is she?'

'Just the same.' Zara threw me a look that would have withered stone then turned her eyes back to the road.

'I know you don't see her.'

'Neither do you.'

'Yes, but I'm never here.'

'And I'm busy.' Zara flicked on the indicator and pulled out to overtake a caravan. 'Come on, Zoe. What's the point? You can't get anything out of her. And it's not like she ever gave us anything.' She flung me another look. 'Be honest. She never did.'

One of my earliest memories was of lying curled up in a damp sleeping bag under a dripping tarpaulin. Creeping forest noises kept me too terrified to sleep but there was no point in crying because there was nobody there to hear. Later I found out where I'd been on that cold, wet night. The Franklin blockade, March 1983. So I was two years old.

There were other memories, too: of being pushed in my stroller down the middle of whatever city we happened to be in for the Palm Sunday marches against nuclear disarmament. Not Brisbane, it wouldn't have been there, because Bjelke Petersen had put an end to street marches years before. International Women's Day rallies with speakers shrieking invective from make-shift platforms; Aboriginal land rights protests in Canberra; protests for gay and lesbian rights in Sydney although I don't think my mother was ever tempted to jump the fence, despite the company she kept.

She was just a protest groupie, my mum, a sad breed of lost souls left over from the hope and hype of the flower power years that had died with the Vietnam war debacle in 1975 and the ignominious end to the Whitlam era later the same year. The only thing Mum had never done was to camp outside the gates of the American air base at Greenham Common. But that was in England and you can't get there by hitching.

We never knew, Zara and I, who our fathers were. My mother used to joke that Zara's father was a Country party cabinet minister and you could believe it, too, the way she'd turned out. Even after we were born, Mum continued to live a gypsy existence, moving aimlessly from one protest to another up and down the east coast.

When we were old enough to go to school, she'd dumped us on our grandparents in Bowen and kept on travelling. The longest she'd ever been in one place had been the six years since her stroke. After our grandparents died and it was obvious Mum wasn't going to get any better, we'd sold the old house and split the proceeds between us. Zara put her share into her four-bedroom rendered brick. I gave mine to Brightsward. We both thought the other was mad.

Zara turned the car into the square of bitumen in front of the nursing home and killed the engine.

'You'll be okay getting home.' It wasn't a question. 'There's a bus every half hour.' She leaned across and opened the door for me. Handed me my stick. 'See you later then.' I stood on the hot bitumen and watched Zara's white car getting the hell out of there.

The nursing home was a long brick building in the middle of a carefully tamed garden. Quiet air. Noisy floors. Too much light. It reminded me of the places I'd been since my accident and I wanted to run. But running was only for dreams. In reality I knew I was lucky to be on my feet.

I sat on the chair by my mother's bed and held her hand. She looked old. Thin. Her thick hair was grey-streaked, tied back with a ribbon. The least Zara could do was to put some henna through it, I thought. Mum would hate the way she looked, if she ever found out.

'Hello, Mum.'

Slowly Mum's head turned on the pillow until her eyes stared into mine.

I took me half an hour to tell Mum everything that had happened since I'd last seen her and there was not even a flicker of an eye lid to show that she'd heard anything of what I said. It was always the same when I came to visit her and I could understand Zara's frustration. But she was my mother and there was still a part of me that needed something from her although I didn't know exactly what it was. Not love. I knew it wasn't love. I'd learned long ago to do without that. In the end I leaned forward, kissed her on the forehead, grabbed my walking stick and left the room.

I was concentrating hard on not slipping on the polished floor of the corridor and I didn't hear the footsteps approaching until I felt a large hand descend onto my shoulder. I turned my head. It was Dr Maddern. A big, ugly man. Kind eyes. Broad, pink hands. Known in Bowen as the bone man because it wasn't their style to call him an orthopaedic surgeon. Semi-retired, he served the retirement village and the nursing home dealing with a steady stream of fractured hips and arthritic complaints. I'd known him ever since I'd broken my leg falling out of a tree, and he was one of the few people on the planet I respected.

'Hello, Zoe. I heard you were back.' Dr Maddern measured his long stride to mine. 'Are you staying around for a while this time? I'm sure Zara is pleased to have you home.'

I shook my head. 'I'm just here until my leg gets better.'

'And then what?'

'I'm going back.'

'To flying?'

'I hope so. Working for Brightsward, anyway.'

'Ah, yes, Brightsward. I've often wondered. The spelling. I mean, is it supposed to be an 'a'? It doesn't really make any sense.'

'It's a play on words,' I said, not for the first time. 'A sward is a patch of grass, see? It kind of represents what we're trying to achieve. And a sword is like the weapon we use to fight for it. I dare say Eric van Eps thought it was quite clever when he thought it up.'

'Eric van Eps?'

'The founder of Brightsward. He made his money out of what we'd call dirty industries these days. Energy. Transport. Refrigeration. He probably created the hole in the ozone layer all by himself.'

'So what made him change his mind?'

'Industrialist to environmentalist? It wasn't such a big step if you hear him tell the story. Once the facts started to emerge about what was happening to the environment he wanted things to change.'

'Have you met him?'

I shook my head. 'He lives in New York. But you get to hear his message often enough when you join the organisation.'

We'd reached the door by now. Dr Maddern pushed it open and held it courteously for me to walk through. He followed me out and we stood at the top of the ramp staring out at the midday heat shimmering off the bitumen in the car park. I wasn't looking forward to stepping out into it. And the thought of the hot, jolting bus ride home almost brought me to tears.

'That leg of yours. It's giving you a bit of pain.' It was as if he'd read my mind.

I turned my head. 'How do you know that?'

'I can see it in your face. There's nothing like bones for nagging, persistent pain. And it seldom kills you. Just drives you crazy.'

'You're right about that.'

'How long since it happened?'

'Three months. I've been in hospital in Argentina.'

'Is it pinned?'

I shook my head. 'The bone was pretty much smashed up. The thing is ... it's worse now than it was when I first did it. It's more … sharp. Stabbing pains. As well as the ache.'

'There are probably some fragments moving about. It's worse now because you're more active. You can come to my outpatients next Wednesday, if you like, and I'll take a look at it.' He reached in his trouser pocket and handed me his card. 'Ring my receptionist and make an appointment. Tell her I said so.'

'Thanks, Dr Maddern.'

'I'm sure I'll be able to make you more comfortable. Now I must be going. I've got patients to see.' He put his big hand on my shoulder. 'How's your mum?'

'Same as always.'

'Pray you never end up like that. It's a living hell.'

'And I haven't helped. Told her all my woes and sorrows.'

'She wouldn't mind. Once a mother, always a mother.'

'She was never much of a mother. Even before.'

TWO

When I got home there was a letter waiting for me. It had the Brightsward logo on the front and was post-marked New York. Zara was standing at the sink peeling potatoes but she turned around and watched me while I turned the envelope over and over in my hands.

'It's from head office. I wonder what they want.'

'Open it and find out.'

I stuck my finger under the flap and ripped upwards.

What they wanted was to tell me they didn't want me any more. They were grateful for what I'd done, sorry about what had happened and hoped I'd find something rewarding to do with the rest of my life. Enclosed with the letter was a bank draft made out in my name. It was a lot of money, more than I'd seen since I took my share of our grandparents' money out of the bank and gave it to Brightsward. Enough to keep me going for a long time. Years, the way I lived.

'So? What does it say?'

I looked up. 'They've paid me off. I didn't think you could get sacked from a volunteer organisation.'

'Let me see.'

Zara wiped her hands on a tea towel and took the bank draft out of my hand. I watched her eyes grow round as she absorbed the amount of money represented by the little row of zeros. Then she looked up and I caught the fleeting expression on her face. Jealousy. It was quite a novelty for Zara to be jealous of me. She dropped the cheque on the table and went back to the sink.

'I don't know what you're getting so upset about.' She picked up a potato and attacked it viciously. 'I wish someone would give me a big fat cheque like that. I'd put it straight on the mortgage, that's what I'd do. But I expect you'll just give it away to some cause or other. It's not like Brightsward is the only one.'

She made it sound like the cats' home or coffee patrol for the winos along the beach front. Pick a cause, any cause. They were all the same to Zara.

I picked up the cheque and shoved it back into the envelope. 'They can stick it up their arse. I don't want it.'

Zara looked up from her peeling. 'Don't be stupid, Zoe. You need something to live on. You can't stay here for ever.'

'I can get a job, can't I?'

'Doing what?'

'Flying helicopters, of course. What the fuck do you think I'm going to do?'

'Don't you swear at me.' Zara pointed her little sharp peeling knife in my direction. 'And I can tell you right now you won't find a job flying helicopters. So you might as well get used to the idea.'

'Why not? There's plenty of work in Queensland. You know that.'

'Because of what happened in Antarctica, that's why not.'

'The accident? What difference does that make?'

I spoke bravely but my heart was sinking rapidly. There was something going on here, something I wasn't going to like when I found out what it was.

'It makes a big difference.' There was an edge of triumph in Zara's voice. 'Because you need a clean record to get a job flying helicopters. And you don't have one any more. Not after what the coroner said.'

'The coroner? What coroner? I didn't know there'd been an inquest.'

'Well, there was.' She threw the little knife into the sink with the potato peelings and walked out of the room. She came back carrying a plastic folder like the ones Tina used for school projects. 'Here you go. Take a look for yourself.'

Inside, held in clear sleeves, were articles cut out of newspapers and magazines, all neat and tidy just the way Zara liked things to be. It seemed I had been a popular girl while I lay in that Buenos Aires hospital waiting for my leg to heal. Harmless most of them. A photograph of the *Astral Traveller* in McMurdo Sound with Mount Erebus in the background. Comments from someone at Brightsward headquarters in New York. A fuzzy picture of my Grade 12 class with a circle around my head. But then, towards the end, the article smaller now that interest in the story had died down, a report on the inquest into Colin's death. Three days in Hobart. And the verdict: pilot error.

I looked up. 'Why didn't you tell me about this before?'

'Because I thought the accident would have knocked all that flying nonsense out of your head, that's why. I never imagined for one moment you'd want to go back to it. And now Brightsward's given you all that money, you can ...'

'I can do what, Zara? Settle down? Is that what you want me to do? Find a man like Derek and settle down?'

'I don't care what you do.' Zara reached out and moved her folder out of harm's way. 'Come on, Zoe, calm down. This isn't doing you any good.'

'Calm down? Calm *down*? Why didn't anyone tell me there was going to be an inquest? Why didn't they ask me what happened?'

'Oh, Zoe, what could you have told them that they didn't already know?'

'The truth. That's what I could have told them.' I stood up, scraping the legs of my chair across Zara's tiled floor. 'I'm going to lie down.'

I don't often cry and I didn't cry then. I just lay on my bed in that hot little room and watched the ceiling fan turn slowly above my head. Of course, Zara was right. I'd never fly again, not with a verdict like that against my name. And maybe I had known about the inquest but the memory was buried somewhere in my mind, along with my memories of the crash itself. I had a sudden image of Nicole, our expedition leader, bringing some papers into the hospital on one of her cheerful visits, along with another bunch of those hot-house lilies that opened slowly, one by one, and stunk the place out for a week.

'It's for a report,' she'd said, rolling her eyes. 'There's always such a mound of paperwork to deal with after an accident. Just what you can remember, Zoe. That is all you can remember, isn't it? Then just sign here, and here, and I'll be on my way.'

And she'd left, swinging her hips up the ward and turning heads as she went. Nicole always managed to look as if she'd just stepped out of a beauty parlour, even when we were on the ship.

Zara was right about something else as well. There was nothing I could have told the inquest that they didn't already know. I'd crashed my helicopter out of a clear blue sky. It wouldn't have taken the coroner very long to reach his verdict. Pilot error. My error. And Colin had died. I'd killed him.

I never knew much about him. Only that he was a university student based at Australia's Casey station during the summer months doing some kind of work on sea temperatures. He was younger than me, small and wiry with an infectious grin and a wicked sense of humour. I met him at McMurdo base on Midsummer Eve. It was an evening of eating, drinking, dressing up and playing silly games.

Sometime after midnight Colin and I had gone outside into the luminous green twilight which was all the night we had at that time of the year. It was cold but not too cold and we had exchanged stories about our Australian childhood summers, the sort of thing you do when you're drunk but not quite drunk enough to go to bed. I had spent mine running wild in the swamps and cane fields around my grandparents' house, listening to the cyclone warnings on the radio and watching the old palm tree by the front gate. My grandfather used to tell me that when the top of the tree touched the ground we were in for a big blow.

Colin had memories of a Brisbane street where three families of boys played endless games of cricket with rubbish bins for wickets and a bat borrowed off someone's dad who'd played club cricket in the glory days of the seventies. What had been glorious about them Colin couldn't remember, only that the price of using the bat was listening to long beery stories about ancient matches, with his mum calling him in for tea the only chance for salvation.

It was the helicopter flight I couldn't get right in my head. I remembered inviting Colin on board the *Astral Traveller*. I remembered offering him a ride in the helicopter. Nicole was planning a big media release to coincide with the launch of Brightsward's new web site and she wanted some shots of a series of ice canyons that had opened up on the Ross shelf. I remembered showing off - hurtling through a canyon the colour of mouthwash while the camera mounted below the helicopter clicked its way through several gigabytes of memory. What I didn't remember was the storm because it had been a clear blue morning when we lifted off from the deck of the ship.

Of course, I knew quite well how quickly the weather could change. I'd been flying in the Antarctic for three months by then and I'd seen the storms sweep in, the winds and the whirling snow obliterating everything within minutes. But this one must have been faster than most because the last thing I remembered was the Dominion Range blocking the horizon, its white peaks gleaming in bright sunshine.

If I'd seen the storm coming, I would have turned back to the ship and I could have spent the rest of the day trying to crack on to the boy with the blue eyes and the ready smile. Instead of which ... But that was the trouble. I couldn't remember anything else. Only lying on the ice with the freezing cold seeping through my torn clothes. The dry snow blowing like grains of sand against my face And the whine of a skidoo fading into the howl of the wind. Which was strange because the Americans had been in a snow-cat, a great ponderous thing that had jerked and juddered its way across the ice with every bump exquisite agony to my shattered leg.

A couple of days later the Americans handed me over to Brightsward and I found myself in a Buenos Aires hospital while I had a series of operations on my shattered leg and waited to find out how many toes I'd lost to frost bite. It had been a long process, watching the black spots of gangrene appear on flesh that had died out there on the ice and it was only a matter of time to see how far they would go.

But, if I'd thought that was bad, this was worse. I stared across the room at the pile of battered boxes containing all the things from my cabin on the *Astral Traveller* and sent on their way to north Queensland. They'd known all along I wasn't going back. So here I lay in my sister's spare room with nothing in front of me but a big, black hole. But first I had to face Dr Maddern and his steel probe poking around inside my leg.

I felt the panic rising sluggishly up my chest towards my heart. I knew it would never get there. I'd had enough operations over the last few months to know the routine. Needle in the back of my hand. The anaesthetist's voice from behind my head. Annoying the way they sat like that where you couldn't see them. The cheerful murmur from the theatre staff. Dr Maddern's eyes above the mask. 'Ready now?' And then the blackness.

Afterwards they gave me morphine and I didn't object. The pain went away to a far corner of my mind and left me to stare out of the window at a patch of sky across which paraded the days, one by one. Bright morning, hazy mid-day, black night. Zara came in every morning with a clean nightie which we threaded past the drip. We were close then when I was weak and didn't mind being mothered. She was a born giver, my sister. It's a pity I've never learned how to take.

On the day of my discharge I was taken in a wheelchair to Dr Maddern's office. He pushed his chair back and looked at me over the top of his glasses.

'Who shot you, Zoe?'

I opened my eyes wide. 'Nobody shot me. It was an accident, I told you that before.'

'That's not what it looks like on your x-ray. Here, I'll show you.' He turned on the light box by his desk and shoved in an x-ray. 'This is your right femur. There's a groove here, see?' He drew his finger down the white line of my bone. 'And then *here* on the other side of the break. You were shot first. Then someone laid into you with a baseball bat. That's what it looks like anyway.'

I peered at the fuzzy grey picture. 'I can't see anything.'

'No, I know, it's not easy to see. But, believe me, it's there. I was in Vietnam, you see, so I've seen plenty like it.' He leaned back in his chair. 'So are you going to tell me what happened?'

I shook my head. 'I don't remember much about it.'

'Tell me what you do remember?'

A patient man, Dr Maddern. I suppose he was used to the dithery old people in the nursing home.

'I don't remember crashing the helicopter, if that's what you mean. I can remember taking off from the ship that morning and the next thing I was lying on the ice with my leg smashed up. Nothing in between.'

Dr Maddern pulled the x-ray out of the light box and flicked off the switch. 'You didn't crash your helicopter, Zoe. Somebody shot it down. And whoever it was didn't want anyone else to find out.' He leaned forward. 'They nearly got away with it, too. It takes a trained eye to see what I saw on your x-ray and the only place you get that kind of training is in a war zone. Who would expect someone like me in a town like Bowen?'

I was silent for a long time while thoughts chased around inside my brain. Dr Maddern, like the good doctor he was, watched me quietly and said nothing.

Finally I said. 'But the inquest. They said it was pilot error.'

'Yes, I read about that.'

'But now you're saying it wasn't my fault? That someone else caused the accident?'

'That's what it looks like to me.'

'So what am I supposed to do now?'

'Go home and rest. That's what you're going to do to begin with. Get that sister of yours to look after you for a few weeks.' Dr Maddern reached out his big pink hand and laid it gently on my knee. 'Then you can decide what you're going to do. I'll be here, if you need to talk.'

'Thanks, Dr Maddern. And thanks for the work you did on my leg. It's beginning to feel better already.'

He grinned. 'There's a bucketful of scraps to show why it should.'

THREE

The skidoo is coming towards us, a racing black shape against the dazzling snow. 'Someone's in a hurry,' says Colin, staring down through the helicopter's curved windscreen. The skidoo skids to a halt in the blue shadow of a snow ridge. We are almost on top of it now. I stare down. Into an eye. The barrel of a gun. Pointing straight at us.

I woke with a start, my body slick with sweat. It was dark outside. I turned over in the narrow bed to check the time. But I knew what time it was. Two o'clock. It was always two o'clock when the nightmares woke me. And now I faced a long restless wait until dawn when I could get up and make myself a cup of tea. I rolled onto my back and stared at the ceiling. It seemed as if my body and mind were in some sort of conspiracy to deny me the sleep I desperately needed. No sooner had the pain in my leg decreased to a dull roar than the nightmares began. Night after night I relived the accident and woke with the echoes of anger, or fear, or grief jangling in my brain. I had even taken to sleeping in the day, something I had never done in my life before. Usually I waited for Zara to go out because I hated the way she approved of my little naps and how she always had the kettle on for a cup of tea when I emerged bleary-eyed a couple of hours later.

However, my body healed, just as Dr Maddern said it would. A couple of weeks after the operation and I was beginning to feel human again. Easter came and went and the dry season arrived. It wasn't cool exactly - it was never cool in Bowen - but the humidity had gone and the sky was an intense blue. Like Antarctica ... But I was trying hard not to think about Antarctica any more. I had enough of it at night when the nightmares came.

News of the whale stranding came six weeks after my operation. I dragged my backpack out from under the bed, left a note for Zara and caught the first bus south. The bus dropped me off at the side of the road with nothing in sight but flat cane fields. It was mid afternoon and the smell of the sea came to me on the breeze that was combing the tops of the young green cane.

Sitting on the bus for so long had made my leg ache and I began walking to ease it. Within five minutes a four wheel drive overtook me and stopped on the gravel shoulder a little way ahead. I saw the driver lean across and open the passenger door. When I caught up I found it was a girl. She had a pale, freckled face, cropped reddish hair and a white tee-shirt stretched across heavy, hard-nippled breasts.

'You look like you could use a ride. Where are you going?' A New York Irish accent. Not what I expected to hear in north Queensland cane country.

'To the whale stranding. Do you know where it is?'

'I'm going there myself.' She reached out her hand. 'I'm Annie Cormack.'

'Zoe Carter.'

'Zoe Carter the helicopter pilot?'

'Not any more.' I climbed awkwardly into the cabin. 'I guess you read about me in the papers.'

'No, I'm with Brightsward. How's the leg now?'

'It's fine, thanks. This is a coincidence, isn't it?'

'Not really. Whales and environmentalists go together pretty good. That's why *you're* here, huh?'

'Well, yes. But I live in Bowen. Just up the coast.'

Annie leaned forward and disengaged the hand brake. 'I've been to Jabaluka. I heard about the whales when I got back to Cairns.'

'I didn't know we ... Brightsward was involved in the Jabaluka protest.'

'We're not officially. I just went to see what's happening

up there. Nuclear energy's going to be a big issue before long ... I guess we go down here.'

Propped against a tree was a beer-carton sign with the word 'WHALES' and an arrow scrawled in thick red pen. Annie wrenched the steering wheel and spun the vehicle onto a dirt track that ran straight between the cane fields.

'I thought nuclear energy had always been an issue.'

'Yeah, but it's kinda been off Brightsward's radar for a while. Now Eric wants it back on the agenda. Enough to send me on a crazy road trip through the Northern Territory to check out the mines. *Damn*, this is a big country!'

'Eric van Eps? You know him?'

Annie turned her head. 'I work with him.'

'What's he like?'

'He's a pretty amazing guy. Making all that money and then turning round and ploughing it back in. At his age.'

'He says he's only cleaning up the mess he helped to make.'

'Oh, yes, I know all that. It's not the real reason though. He's got a granddaughter, did you know that?'

I shook my head.

'Not many people do. I have always regarded her as the single most influential female on the planet.' She flicked me a grin, then turned her eyes back to the road. 'Sad, really, for those of us that do the real work.'

'Why influential?'

'She's the reason Eric van Eps pours his money into Brightsward. He wants to make sure there's going to be a world for her to live in.'

'How old is she?'

'She's nineteen, our Madeleine. A doped-out air-head with one of the world's richest men twisted around her little finger.'

'Sounds as if you don't like her much.'

Another grin. 'You got that right. But I know how important she is to Brightsward. And, if Eric succeeds in making a world fit for his precious Madeleine to live in, there'll be a world for the rest of us, too, won't there? Nothing wrong with that.'

The road ended in a rough gravel square on which half a dozen cars were parked untidily. A galvanised iron water tank and a standard issue National Parks toilet block stood on a patch of scruffy grass. A track led over the dunes.

It was chaos on the beach. The tide was full. Upwards of fifty small black whales wallowed in the inshore breakers. Someone had a fire going and the sharp scent of wood smoke mingled with the strong fishy stench given off by the whales. People were busy with buckets or standing chest deep in the water, buffeted by the wind-driven surf, as they heaved and pushed at the inert bodies. Further out two fishing boats rode the swell.

It was when I entered the water that I discovered what toes were for. I had lost three on one foot and I found it difficult to maintain my balance in the wet, shifting sand. Within minutes I had fallen twice and was thoroughly soaked. Although the water was warm, the cool afternoon breeze quickly chilled my body. I felt the beginning of an insistent protest from my injured leg. An elderly woman with a lined face and thin grey hair took great delight in my difficulties. She was balancing easily in the rough water with a whale clasped to her bosom like a gigantic baby.

'Perhaps you'd better join the bucket brigade, deary,' she shouted at me over the sound of the surf. 'You're not much use out here.'

I staggered back onto the beach and sat by the fire with my head between my hands. I looked around for my back-pack where my painkillers were.

'This what you're looking for?' Annie handed me my bag, followed by a plastic mug of tea. 'I didn't know about your toes. Frostbite?'

I nodded. Sipped the tea gratefully. 'There's an old woman out there who thinks it's funny I can't stand up in the surf.'

'She doesn't know what she's talking about. Stupid old cow.'

Late in the afternoon a council tractor laboured up the beach and removed the dead whales and by nightfall the rest lay stranded by the tide, puffing and sighing, with the moonlight gleaming off their wet skin. A number of people were out on the wet sand keeping them company. The rest of us were up on the beach eating bread and sausages and talking in low voices, exchanging experiences. Annie told the group about me, made me show them where my toes were missing and - reluctantly - the purple, puckered scars on my leg.

As a consequence, I scored a joint which was passed to me out of the darkness by a hand with black hairs growing on the backs of the fingers. It was the first smoke I'd had for months and it took me back instantly to the deck of the *Astral Traveller* and the smell of the ice. I offered it to Annie but she shook her head.

'I'm going to help with the whales.'

I smoked in silence, sharing the joint with the owner of the hand. Finally I flicked the butt away and watched the tiny red glow spiral away into the darkness. I lay down in the warm sand with my hands behind my head.

Annie's face loomed above me. 'You okay?'

'Yeah, I'm fine.'

She sat down next to me. 'I'm glad I met you, Zoe. I'll be able to tell Eric you're doing okay. He was worried about you after the accident.'

I sat up and wrapped my arms around my legs. 'It wasn't an accident, Annie. I was shot.'

'Shot?' Annie turned her head abruptly. 'How do you know that?'

'A friend of mine ... a doctor ... found it on an x-ray. He said I'd been shot and then someone laid into my leg so nobody would find out.'

'Are you sure about this?'

'He's sure. It isn't that easy to see if you don't know what you're looking for.'

'So he could be wrong?'

'He could be, but I don't think he is.' I leaned forward urgently. 'Look, Annie, this is a big deal for me. There was an inquest in Hobart, did you know that? They returned a verdict of pilot error. Do you think I'm going to get another job flying helicopters after that? And then Brightsward tosses me on the scrap heap. No explanation, just a big fat cheque, thank you very much and see you later.'

'Is that how you saw it? Because that's not how it was meant.' Annie's hard hand came down on my shoulders. 'You were injured working for us. Why shouldn't we make sure you're all right?'

I shook my head. 'It doesn't make any difference why you gave me the money, Annie. My life's wrecked. Totally wrecked. And, if it was my fault, then fair enough. But if someone else was responsible, I'd like to know who it was.'

'So what are you going to do?'

'There's nothing much I can do.' I turned my head and stared out at the dark ocean. 'All I've got is a fuzzy line on an x-ray. I think I'd need a bit more than that to get an inquest reopened.'

'No, I didn't mean that.' Annie removed her hand. The cold breeze attacked the warm patch she'd left behind. 'Listen, Zoe, are you still interested in working for Brightsward?'

'Yes, of course I am. Brightsward and flying, they're the only things I care about.'

'It won't be flying. The *Astral Traveller*'s in Buenos Aires undergoing maintenance. And Eric's not well.'

'What's wrong with him?'

'Nobody's really sure. But we're scaling back operations until he gets better.'

'I'll do anything. It doesn't matter what it is.'

'Okay, I'll see what I can do.'

Annie leaned forward and put her hand high up on my thigh.

'Annie.'

'What?'

'I'm straight.'

She grinned. 'Okay. Worth a try.'

It took me a while to fall asleep. The sand was hard and I couldn't get my leg into a comfortable position. A cold wind blew along the beach, stirring up the ashes of the fire. The beached whales sighed in the darkness and exuded their fishy smells. And I guess I'd been lying in soft beds for so long I'd forgotten what it was like to curl up in a sleeping bag and sleep under the stars. In the middle of the night I got up and joined the bucket brigade working in the messy chop of the incoming tide, then I returned to my sleeping bag, cold and exhausted.

Towards morning, I fell into a deep sleep. Blackness for a while, then the dream again. But different this time. The scream of the wind. Agony from my shattered leg. I am lying on the snow staring at Colin's face and he is staring back. Only not with his eyes alone. There is a round, red hole in the middle of his forehead, seeping blood thickly into the freezing air.

When I awoke it was full daylight. The tide was up and everyone was in the water with what was left of the whales. Annie's sleeping bag had gone from its place by the fire. I stayed until the last of the bodies had been dragged away, then I packed my bag and began the long trek through the cane fields to the highway. I hitched a ride to Bowen with some bloke who wanted to tell me about his new baby daughter and was dropped off near the jetty just before midnight.

It was Sunday night and the coffee patrol was making its way along the narrow strip of parkland that fronted the beach. I recognised the tall lanky frame of Dr Maddern and lifted my hand in answer to his shouted greeting. Someone had given me a joint as a parting gift and I went down onto the sand to smoke it. The tide was up and the reflections from the street lights were swilling up and down in the dark water. After a while Dr Maddern climbed down the rocks and folded up his body next to mine.

'Back from the whale stranding?'

I turned my head. 'How did you know where I was?'

He smiled. 'I saw your sister in town. Although I probably could have guessed for myself where you'd gone. It's the kind of thing I'd expect you to do.'

'I don't suppose Zara was too pleased about it. She's trying to reform me again. Give up on Brightsward. Give up on flying. Get myself a proper job. Talking of which …' I took a long drag from the joint and blew blue smoke into the darkness. 'I met someone from Brightsward at the whale stranding. Annie Cormack. She said she might be able to find me a job.'

'Not flying helicopters.'

'No, not flying helicopters. But anything would be better than hanging around here going slowly mad.'

I inhaled deeply and flicked the butt away into the darkness.

'You shouldn't smoke that stuff, you know.'

'Why not? It's good for pain, you know that.' I grinned. 'You should give some to the old ladies in the nursing home. It would do them the world of good.'

'Are you still having trouble with the leg? I can give you something, if you are.'

I grinned. 'No thanks, Doc. That shit's better than any stuff you can give me. Anyway I'm not having much pain, not any more.'

'You're still looking tired. Any problems sleeping?'

'It's not so much sleeping. I don't have any problems getting to sleep. Only I've been having nightmares. And they wake me up.'

'Every night?'

'Most nights.'

'What are they about?'

'They're about the crash. Over and over again.'

'You told me you didn't remember anything about the crash.'

'I don't. I still don't. Except … Dr Maddern, do you think my nightmares could be memories coming up to the surface? They seem very real. And it's like I'm filling in the gaps, you know? Each dream adds a little bit more to the picture.'

'Well, I'm no expert but I don't see why not.' He leaned forward and tapped me gently on the side of my head. 'It's all in there somewhere, Zoe. Just because you can't remember it doesn't mean it isn't there.'

'Last night I dreamt about Colin. I haven't dreamt about him before.'

'Colin ... he was the person who died in the crash?'

I nodded. 'They never found his body. Nobody knows what happened to him.'

'What did you dream, Zoe?' Dr Maddern's voice was very gentle.

'I dreamt he had a red hole in the middle of his forehead.' I felt a hard lump of tears at the back of my throat and swallowed them away.

'A bullet wound.' Dr Maddern was back to making statements again.

'Someone shot my 'copter down,' I said. 'Remember? You saw it on my x-ray'

'Yes, yes, I remember *that*. But this is something else again. The bullet that struck your leg was fired by someone who wanted to crash your helicopter. You can disable a helicopter with one bullet through the rotors. Or maybe they just wanted to disable *you*. Either way it was the same result. But a bullet ... here.' He pointed to a spot between his eyes. 'That's a different matter altogether. That's murder.'

I opened my eyes wide. 'Murder? But why?'

Dr Maddern cocked an eye brow in my direction. 'Well, that's the big question, isn't it? Someone takes a pot shot at the Brightsward helicopter, it could have been anything. Maybe you strayed too close to a sensitive area and it was a warning to keep away. Brightsward has a reputation for poking its nose where it doesn't belong. But, from what you've just told me, this was a deliberate targeting. Not of you, or your helicopter.'

'Of Colin.'

'Precisely. What was Colin doing in the Antarctic, Zoe?'

'He was taking samples of sea water, that's all I know. He spent his days staring down a microscope at bacteria in a petri dish. That's why I took him up in the helicopter, so he could see something real for a change.'

'He was a scientist?'

'A student.'

'An Australian?'

I nodded. 'A Brisbane boy.'

'And you don't know why he was taking these samples?'

'He told me he was looking for evidence of climate change.'

'So why would someone want to kill a Brisbane student in Antarctica doing research into climate change?'

I shook my head. 'I have no idea. But I'm going to find out. Because the person who killed Colin destroyed my life, too. It's not just my leg, though that's bad enough. Everything I trained for and worked for, all the things that were important to me, died on the ice that day.' I reached out and grabbed his arm. His skin felt warm under my hand. 'But, if I can find Colin's killer I'll be able to prove my helicopter was shot down deliberately. Don't you see? It's my best chance to get back to flying again. Probably my only chance.'

'So what are you going to do?'

'You reckon Colin was killed because of his research?'

'I can't think of another explanation.'

'And he was a student, right? A university student.'

'So you said.'

'So I'll go to Brisbane. Find his university. Find the people who knew him. Worked with him. Ask them what he was doing down there in the Antarctic.'

Dr Maddern nodded his head. 'That sounds like a good idea. And this girl from Brightsward … Anne, did you say her name was?

'Annie. Annie Cormack. What about her?'

'Didn't she say she was going to find you some work?'

I thought of Annie Cormack's big, hard hand squeezing my thigh.

'Yeah, well, let's just wait and see, eh? In the meantime, I'm off to Brisbane. Do something useful for a change.'

For a while we sat in silence listening to the hush of the waves on the sand and the occasional plop of a fish somewhere out in the darkness. The air was cool and dry. The sort of air that would make a frost somewhere other than Bowen. Then Dr Maddern unfolded his long body from the sand. 'Time I headed home. I've got an early start in the morning.' He dusted the sand off his hands and held one out. 'Come on, I'll pull you up.'

We climbed up the rocks into the yellow glare of a street lamp. The beach front was empty. Even the drunks had wandered off looking for somewhere to spend the night. The only moving thing was a thin dog trotting purposefully in and out of the pools of light.

'Where's your car?' I asked.

'I'm walking.' He tapped his chest. 'Good for the old ticker. But what about you? Do you want me to find you a taxi?'

I shook my head. 'No, it's okay. I think I'll walk, too. It'll give me time to think.'

He held out his hand. 'Well, good bye for now. Take care of that leg of yours. And keep in touch, eh? Let me know how you're getting along.'

I reached out and we shook hands. 'Yeah, thanks, Doc. Thanks a lot.'

He turned away and I watched his tall, lean body as he made his way along the empty footpath until he was lost in darkness.

FOUR

It took me longer than I expected to walk home from the beach front and the sky was washed with grey by the time I turned into the narrow road that led to my sister's house. I didn't hear the car coming up behind me. The headlights, feeble in the dawn light, gave me just enough warning to dive off the roadway as the car swept by. It was Derek's car.

The fall winded me and set off the jangling ache in my leg that the long walk had aroused. I picked myself up and limped towards to the house. The car was parked under the car port and Derek was crouched on the passenger side running his fingers along a deep gouge in the front panel. The passenger door was torn and crumpled like crepe paper.

He looked up. 'You okay?'

'No, I'm not okay. You nearly fucking killed me.'

'You shouldn't have been walking in the middle of the road.'

'And you shouldn't have been driving so fast.'

'Yeah, okay, you've made your point.' Derek stood up wearily. 'Come on, Zoe, don't give me a hard time. I've had enough for one night.'

'I can see that.' I ran my hands over the twisted metal of the door. 'What *happened*?'

'I hit a roo. It jumped straight out in front of me.' He flicked me a look to see how I'd taken it. 'I went down to the beach front to get a breath of fresh air. I'd spent too long in front of the computer.'

'I wish I'd seen you. You could have given me a lift home.'

He was lying, of course. Wherever else Derek Antonino had been that night it had not been the Bowen beach front.

But I knew I wouldn't say anything to Zara. I have never been married so I don't know what goes on inside a relationship like that. And anything that was going on between my sister and brother-in-law was their business, not mine. Besides, I was leaving in the morning.

I spent my first night in Brisbane in a backpackers' hostel in Roma Street and the following morning, following the instructions of the young girl behind the desk, I caught a bus to St Lucia. The bus filled quickly with noisy, strap-hanging students with puddles of untidy bags at their feet. At the university it stopped in an open space surrounded by a miscellany of odd-shaped buildings. The hordes of students galloped off with me in their midst. They all knew where they were going and went there before I had a chance to ask anyone for help. My leg was aching and it didn't help that it was my own fault. I still wasn't used to having Brightsward's money in the bank so I'd ignored my sister's advice and travelled to Brisbane by bus, instead of taking a nice short plane ride that would have cost twice as much but saved my leg the agony it was in now.

Across the road from the bus stop I found a refectory hidden under a square library building. I bought myself a cup of what they said was coffee to wash down some painkillers, then looked around for somewhere to sit in the noisy, crowded space. I hooked my stick over my arm and limped towards a table by the window which was occupied by a young man who was devouring a pie drowned in thick brown gravy. In front of him a pile of books and papers threatened to topple onto his plate.

'Excuse me, do you mind if I share your table?'

He looked up, then scrambled to his feet. 'Here, let me help.'

He was a big man, running to fat, with the kind of skin you get if you stay indoors too much. Long hair in a pony tail, baggy jeans, shaggy brown jumper. He had 'student' written all over him, though he was closer to my own age than the people I'd shared the bus with.

'Name's Martin,' he said, when he had settled me to his

satisfaction, put my stick where I could find it and placed my coffee on the table in front of me.

'I'm Zoe Carter.'

He reached his big hand across the table. 'Pleased to meet you, Zoe. What are you studying?'

I shook my head. 'I'm not a student.'

He gulped a lump of pie. 'So what are you doing on campus?'

'I'm looking for someone. It's just that ...' I waved my hand at the unfamiliar world beyond the grimy window. 'I had no idea the place was so *big*.'

He looked up. 'You a country gel?'

I nodded. 'I'm from Bowen.'

He nodded. 'It's a bit daunting when you first get here.' Another mouthful of pie. 'So who are you trying to find?'

I hesitated. 'Martin, you're a student, aren't you?'

'Doing a PhD.' He grinned. 'I'll be Dr Martin one day. Like the boots.'

The joke flew over the top of my head. 'Are you a scientist?'

'No, doing arts.' He indicated the pile of old books. 'You don't find many of us about. We're a dying breed.'

'The person I'm looking for was ... is a scientist.' I dropped my head and stared down at the murky brown liquid in my mug. 'I want to find out about his research.'

'Why don't you ask him?'

I looked up. 'Not so easy. I met him in the Antarctic.'

'The Antarctic? What were you doing down there?'

'Flying helicopters for Brightsward.'

'Flying helicopters? I've never met a gel that could fly a helicopter before.'

I smiled. 'Well, you've met one now. Not that I fly any more. Not since I hurt my leg.'

'That's no good.' Martin finished the last of his pie and pushed the plate away. 'So what do you want to know?'

I hesitated. Martin seemed like a nice bloke but that didn't mean I could trust him with the truth, which meant I would have to lie to him, if I wanted his help But lying was not something that came naturally to me. In fact, I was hopeless at it.

Finally I said, 'Brightsward was in Antarctica gathering evidence on global warming. Colin ... my friend ... was working on the same thing, but from a scientific point of view. I ... I'm trying to tie the two together. His work and our work, you know?'

'You're writing a paper?'

'Well, yeah,' I said, sliding gratefully off the hook. 'I'm writing an article on global warming.'

Martin pulled the band out of his pony tail, dragged his fingers through his hair and tied it back up again. 'What was he working on specifically?'

'Sea temperatures.'

'Okay. So ... climatology? Oceanography?'

I shook my head. 'I have no idea.'

He stood up and gathered his books under his arm. 'We'll try Parnell. Across the Great Court.'

'You don't have to come with me.'

'No, it's okay. I'm teaching later this afternoon but I've got an hour or so before then.'

'What do you teach?'

He pulled a face. 'I tutor the First Years. That's what us poor postgrads have to do to earn our meagre crust.' Martin put his hand under my elbow and heaved me gently to my feet. He handed me my stick and picked up my back pack. 'Come on, then.'

Leaving me to follow as best I could, he pushed his way out of the refectory and loped up a flight of stone steps. Through a lobby hung with scrappy notice boards then out of another door that lead to sandstone cloisters surrounding a wide space of dry grass. By the door, chip packets swirled. Martin took off across the scruffy grass to a building on the other side of the court. Two shallow steps and into a dark foyer smelling of floor polish and old mice. Students lounged outside the bright shell of a lecture theatre, bags in a huddle on the blotchy linoleum floor.

Martin took the wide marble stairs two at a time and I followed. A gloomy corridor opened into a chilly reception area. Behind a high wooden counter sat an elderly woman with rimless glasses and an expression of habitual annoyance.

Martin blocked the light with his bulk and waited to be noticed.

Finally, 'Can you tell me if there is anyone in the school researching sea temperatures?'

His eager puppy expression was having no visible effect on the ice woman behind the counter.

'Anyone in particular?'

'A student. Colin …' Martin turned to me.

'Wilson,' I said. 'Colin Wilson.

A nasty odour seemed to pass under the woman's nose. She was clearly no fan of students of any description. Being helpful was also against her nature because there was a brief silence before she said, 'Try Dr Westcott's lab. Upstairs.'

The 'upstairs' was an added bonus for which Martin was truly grateful.

'What an old cow,' I said as I followed him back to the stairs. 'Martin, slow *down*.'

Martin slackened his pace. 'Sorry. I forgot about your leg.'

'It's not my leg. It's my legs. They're much shorter than yours.'

'There are a lot of old dragons like her at the university.' He jerked his head in the direction of the reception area.

'Why do they work here, then? If they hate students so much?'

Another grin. 'You picked up on that, then?'

Martin galloped up the next flight of stairs and I galloped after him, something I knew I would regret later in the day. But there was no joy upstairs. We found the lab but it was empty. There were a couple of students in a cold little room crouched over an electric heater and eating pizza out of a cardboard box. They hadn't heard of Colin, or any other student who had gone to the Antarctic. They made it quite clear we were disturbing their lunch, so we left them to it. Outside it had started raining.

Martin huddled into his brown jumper. 'No luck there, then. Come on, we'll try Angela.' He grinned down at me. 'She's *our* dragon lady.'

Angela was fortyish, curly haired, and was wearing a

green velvet jacket I would've killed to own. Photos of kids and dogs jostled for space on the busy notice board above her desk. She looked up from the computer and smiled at Martin as if she had been waiting all morning for him to show up.

'How's it going, Martin? Are you writing up yet?'

'No, not yet, Angela. End of the year I should start. This is Zoe. She's looking for a student.'

Angela's smile turned its warm beam onto me. 'Doing ancient history, like Martin?'

'He's not one of ours,' said Martin. 'He's studying sea temperatures.'

'Have you tried Physical Sciences? That would be your best bet.'

'We've just come from there.'

'Does he have a name? This student of yours?'

'Colin,' I said. 'Colin Wilson.'

Angela bent her head to her computer. 'Let's have a look, then. I'm not supposed to do this, you know. I could get into terrible trouble.' There was silence while she clicked through the screens. 'Here he is. School of Molecular Sciences. Doing a PhD. Or he was. Looks like he's not enrolled this semester.'

'That's odd,' said Martin, scribbling down the details on a scrap of paper. 'What've bugs got to do with sea temperatures, I wonder? 'Thanks, Angela. See you later.'

'Yeah, see you, Martin.' Angela looked up from her screen and gave him another one of her exclusive smiles.

'Bugs?' I followed Martin out of the office.

'Bacteria, viruses, all that jazz. That's what they do over there. Look, Zoe, I've got to go and teach now. D'you think you can find it by yourself? It's building 78. Down by the river.'

'I should be okay.' I stuck out my hand. 'Thanks for everything, Martin. I really appreciate your help.'

Martin shifted his pile of books to his other arm and shook my hand.

'You're welcome. I hope you find what you're looking for.'

I watched him lope away through the rain, his shoulders hunched into his disreputable jumper. Another time, another place and I wouldn't have let him go without the promise of a phone call at least. Not just because he knew his way around the campus and I didn't. But there was something about him that I really liked.

A new building this time. Warm inside. I took the lift to the third floor and found a long, grey counter with a girl behind it. Young. Pale skinned. Bored to tears.

'I'm looking for Colin Wilson's supervisor.'

The girl said nothing. She stared at me with her vacant blue eyes and I had a momentary panicked thought that I'd asked for the wrong thing. I wished Martin was still there with his easy understanding of this strange world. But then she spoke.

'Professor McRae. Next floor. But you won't find him.' She glanced at a clock. 'He's teaching until three.'

'Can I wait?'

'If you like.'

There was a room at the end of the corridor with chairs surrounding a low table piled with dog-eared magazines. I sat down and stretched out my leg. Watched the rain slide down the window. People came in and took food out of the fridge. Made coffee and sniffed the milk. A phone shrilled insistently somewhere close by but nobody answered it. After a while I felt myself sliding into sleep.

Finally three o'clock came and I climbed a flight of stairs to the next floor. A young girl in a white lab coat directed me to Professor McRae's office, a small room off the main lab. He was stout, red-whiskered and not exactly welcoming. He turned his seat a half circle away from his desk, hoisted one bushy eye brow and waited for me to justify disturbing him in his lair.

'I'm Zoe Carter from Brightsward.' Not strictly true, but close enough for now. 'I wondered if I could talk to you about Colin Wilson?'

'Colin Wilson?' Interest now in the pale blue eyes. 'He's dead, you know that I suppose?'

'Yes, I know. I'm interested in his research.'

'Are you indeed? And why might that be?'

'I'm trying to get some sort of a picture of what he was doing in Antarctica,' I said. 'You see, I was with him when he died.'

'In the helicopter?' Professor McRae's pale eyes bulged slightly.

'Yes.'

'The Brightsward helicopter?'

'Yes. I was the pilot.'

The chair came round full circle. Professor McRae dropped his elbows on his knees and leaned forward. 'What was Brightsward doing in the Antarctic, Miss Carter?'

'Looking for evidence of global warming.'

'Colin was doing the same thing. But not by flying helicopters over the ice searching for cracks.'

'He told me he was studying sea temperatures.'

It was an effort to keep my voice steady in the face of this man's relentless rudeness. But then Professor McRae seemed to arrive at some sudden internal decision.

'Sit down, young lady, sit down.' He leaned forward and pushed a pile of papers off the chair next to his desk. 'Colin went down to Antarctica to study bacteria in the Southern Ocean. He was looking for a marker for temperature change.'

'A ... a marker?'

'I'll explain it to you. Bacteria are sensitive little critters. Most people don't know that. They think they're tough because they live everywhere. And it's true, bacteria grow everywhere in the world but each species inhabits its own particular niche. And if a niche isn't to their liking, they stop living there. They die, dwindle or decamp. In short, they disappear. Let me show you what I mean.'

Professor McRae searched on his desk and came up with a sheath of photographs. A bore in the middle of sparse country gushing boiling water into a yellow-tinged pool. A sluggish stream running away thick with green algae.

'This is the work Colin did for his Honours thesis. We're writing it up as a paper, which is why the photos are on my desk. Were writing it up,' he corrected himself. He placed his finger on one of the photographs. 'This is an artesian bore in western Queensland. As you can see, the water reaches the surface at a very high temperature. The yellow stain is evidence of the growth of what we call hyperthermophilic bacteria. As the water drains away, it cools down and these particular organisms are no longer evident.'

I leaned forward and picked up the photo. 'So these bacteria can tolerate hot water?'

'Not just tolerate it. They absolutely love it. The hotter the better for these little critters.'

'But they don't like cooler water?'

'Correct.'

'So what's the connection between these bacteria and what Colin was doing in the Antarctic?'

Professor McRae turned his pale blue eyes towards me. 'Colin was looking around for a topic for his PhD. He was interested in these thermophilic bacteria. He wanted to use them to develop a test for measuring temperature variation in water.'

'Because where they grow tells you something about the temperature of the water?'

'That's right. Of course, the most interesting and critical temperature variation in the world today is in the Southern Ocean ...'

'... because it measures global warming,' I said, suddenly understanding. 'He wanted to find a bug that would die out if the temperature in the ocean rose too high.'

Professor McRae nodded. 'Exactly. Of course, getting to Antarctica is not easy but Colin was lucky. He found an institute in the US that was funding this type of research and they were interested in his work. They gave him a scholarship to go to Antarctica and look for his ... his bug, as you call it.'

'And did he find it?'

I don't know what he found, Miss ... er,' he said, 'because I don't have any of his data.'

'His ... data?'

'The results of his experiments.'

'Didn't he send them to you?'

'Why should he send them to me? I was his supervisor not

his nursemaid.' Professor McRae rolled his r's, a remnant of some remote Scottish ancestry.

'So what happened to them?'

'I don't know what happened to them, Miss Carter. He didn't send them here because I've already had the IT boys check his computer. I wanted to take a look at what he'd come up with to see if there was anything worth writing up.'

'Maybe he sent them home,' I said, thinking of Martin and his piles of books.

'Home? Oh, you mean *his* home. Aye, maybe he did. Tell you what ...' Professor McRae began rummaging among the papers on his desk. 'Why don't you pay a visit to Colin's father? Ask him if he's got his data. He's a nice chap. Ex-policeman. I met him at Colin's memorial service. Ah, here we are.' He reached for a block of post-it notes and scribbled a number. 'Mention my name when you call. I'm sure he'll be most helpful.' He ripped the note off the block and handed it to me. 'Now remember, if Mr Wilson gives you Colin's data, you bring it straight back here to me, all right?' He lifted his lip in a smile, showing discoloured teeth. 'If I can get a paper out of it, I'll put Colin as first author. That would be something to make his family proud, eh?'

'Okay.' I stood up. 'Thanks for your help.'

But I'd lost him. Before I reached the door he'd turned his back to me and was engrossed in his computer screen. A pile of papers slid silently onto the floor and disappeared under his desk.

Outside it was still raining. The street lights were on as if heralding the end of the gloomy day. Martin was standing at the bottom of the steps with his pile of old books held in his arms like a bulky baby. With the raindrops clinging to his brown jumper he looked like an old dog kicked out of the house. Then he turned his head and there were those beautiful dark eyes.

'You forgot your bag.' At his feet was my backpack containing everything I owned.

I felt my heart skip a beat. 'Where did I leave it?'

He grinned. 'Angela's been looking after it for you.'

'Thanks, Martin. Thanks a lot.' I picked up the bag and slid it onto my shoulder. 'I hadn't even realised it was gone.'

'How did you get on in there? Did you find what you were looking for?'

I shrugged. 'It would help if I knew what that was.'

'So now what?'

'I'm staying in a hostel in the city. Could you point me in the direction of the bus stop?'

'Look, Zoe, why don't you come back to my place?' He hefted the pile of old books under one arm and reached for my elbow in a gesture that would normally have made me wild with rage. 'It's not far and I've got a spare bed you can sleep in. Don't take it the wrong way, but you look like you've done enough walking for one day.'

He was right. I was almost dead on my feet. I allowed Martin to lead me to the bus stop and onto a bus where he found me a seat and guarded me with his big, bulky body. At the end of the short journey I made a detour into a bottle shop and bought two bottles of half-decent red wine and a block of chocolate, all of which were as essential to my survival just then as the promise of a warm bed. It was almost dark when we reached Martin's house in a street sloping down to a ferry stop and the dull green glint of the river. The house was a kind of retro 30s English brick, with a steep tiled roof and wooden window frames sporting an odd collection of glass and plywood. The wrought iron gate was wedged half open on a cracked concrete path. Behind a torn flyscreen, the front door was unlocked.

I followed him through a dingy living room inhabited by an old-fashioned lounge suite into the kitchen at the back of the house. A sink, a stove, a rusty fridge. A large table with carved legs held a dirty plate almost buried under piles of books and papers. Above the table, stuck up with blu-tack, a picture of a beautiful young man with a thick mane of hair springing from a peak in the middle of his forehead. It had been downloaded from the Internet and enlarged too much so his face was divided into pixellated squares and blocks.

'Cup of tea?' Martin added his books to the pile on the table.

'No, thanks. I'm going to open the wine, if that's okay with you. Who's he?'

Martin followed the direction of my gaze. 'That's Alexander. The Great,' he added, in case I didn't know who he was talking about. 'The love of my life.' And, in response to my startled look. 'Alexander the Great is the topic for my PhD. His army, to be more specific.'

'One of these days I'll find out what a PhD is.' I unscrewed the cap on the bottle of wine, found two glasses that were slightly cleaner than the rest and poured a generous slug into each. 'Here you go. You do drink, don't you?'

He grinned. 'Not very often. I can't afford it.'

I took a gulp of wine then stared at him over the rim of my glass. 'Well, tonight's my shout. To say thanks for everything. I'll even cook dinner if you've got anything to eat in your fridge.'

The only things in Martin's freezer were some plastic-wrapped packets of grey meat he said were lamb, but I managed to produce a sort of casserole with an old onion, a couple of worn out carrots and a generous slosh of wine from the first bottle. While it was cooking, I succumbed to Martin's invitation and soaked myself in a hot bath which was the closest thing to bliss I'd known since I injured my leg.

Martin engulfed the food in silence, mashed his potatoes into the gravy and wiped his plate with a slice of bread. I assumed he'd enjoyed it. We shoved the dirty dishes in the sink and went into the front room where Martin made me lie on the damp, beer-smelling couch. He covered me with an old quilt off the spare bed, then sat himself untidily in one of the armchairs and began doling out equal shares of the chocolate I'd bought in the bottle shop. I was sleepy and content. For once my leg wasn't aching, numbed in equal measures by the hot bath and the alcohol. I didn't think I was going to be awake for much longer.

It was strange to feel so much at home in a house I'd been in for a couple of hours. With a man I'd known for barely a day. And it wasn't just the bath and the dinner and the wine and the chocolate. And the sound of the wet night blustering outside the window. There was more to it than that.

'It's bad for arthritis, you know,' I said, remembering Dr Maddern. 'Chocolate,' I explained to Martin's puzzled face. 'I'll have to remember when I get older.'

Martin reached out and broke off another row of chocolate. 'Just get your share now, that's what I reckon.'

'Martin?' I reached out and caught the piece of chocolate Martin chucked across the table to me.

'Mmm?'

'I need somewhere to live while I'm in Brisbane. Can I stay here? I'll pay rent.'

'Do the cooking and you can stay here for free.'

I shook my head. 'I'm not really the cooking type.'

'How long are you going to stay?'

'I'm not sure. A couple of weeks?'

'It doesn't matter anyway. You can stay as long as you like.' He grinned. 'And, if you ever feel like cooking again, I'm not going to stop you.'

'Thanks, Martin. Thanks a lot.'

FIVE

I woke to bright sunshine and the sound of a City Cat ferry surging energetically up the river. My mobile phone was shrilling urgently from under my pillow. I scrabbled for it, stared blankly at the illuminated screen, and hit the button. It was my sister.

'Hi, Zoe, how are you?'

'I was asleep.'

'But it's nine o' clock. What are you doing in bed at this hour of the day?' Which was Zara's way of reminding me I was wasting my life.

'What do you want, Zara?'

'I've got some bad news for you. Dr Maddern's dead.'

I sat up and clutched the phone against my ear. 'Dead? What happened?'

'He was hit by a car.'

'When?'

A tiny silence. Then, 'It was the night before you left for Brisbane.'

'The night before I left? I saw him that night.' I remembered Dr Maddern's tall, lean body walking away from me along the empty street. 'So why have you left it 'til now to let me know?'

'I'm sorry, Zoe. It's been really difficult.' There was another pause, then my sister continued, 'Derek's been to the police station.'

'Has he been arrested?' It was an attempt at humour but my heart was pounding. I was thinking of Derek in the dawn light fingering the deep gouges in the front panel of their car.

'No, of course he hasn't been arrested, Zoe.' My sister's voice had a hard edge to it. 'But the car's in the panel beaters and the cops wanted to know what happened to it.'

'He told me he'd hit a 'roo.'

'What time did Derek get home that night, Zoe? He said you both got home at the same time'

Well, it was dawn. Four o'clock in the morning. He'd been out all night.

'Yeah, we did.' Cautiously.

'He said it was about two,' persisted Zara. 'Is that right?'

I thought quickly. It could have been two if I'd gone straight home instead of sitting on the beach smoking that joint. And the only other person who knew about that was Dr Maddern.

'Two? Yeah, that'd be about right.'

I listened to myself lying for my brother-in-law and wondered why I was doing it. Wondered what I was covering up. And I didn't say anything about being on the beach front that night. Not because it would wreck Derek's alibi. I didn't care about that. I just didn't want to get involved in whatever my brother-in-law had been up to. Let Zara sort it out. She was the one who was married to him.

'Will the police want to talk to me, do you think?'

'I shouldn't think so.' Zara's voice has lost its edge now. 'You keep in touch, okay?'

I ended the call and shoved the phone back under my pillow. I rolled onto my back and stared at the ceiling. Thought about that gentle man, dead because someone had been driving too fast. Someone who might turn out to be my sister's husband. And it got worse. Because Dr Maddern was the only other person in the world who knew about Colin's murder. If my search for Colin's data lead me nowhere, what would I do then?

There was a knock on the door and Martin elbowed his way in, balancing a full mug in one hand. 'Here you go. Thought you might need these.' His other hand held two white tablets. 'They're only Panadol. I didn't know if you had something stronger.'

I struggled to sit up. 'No, that's fine. Thanks.'

Martin dropped the two white tablets into my outstretched hand and dumped the mug of tea on the table by the bed. 'You okay?'

I stared up at him. 'What do you mean?'

A sheepish grin. 'I've got three sisters. I know when a gel's upset.'

'I've had some bad news from home. Dr Maddern ... the doctor who fixed up my leg. He's been killed in a hit and run.'

'That's no good.'

'He's going to be missed, that's for sure. There aren't too many doctors like him in a place like Bowen.'

The words echoed in my mind like the jangle of a distant bell.

'What's up?'

'Nothing. Just going crazy, that's all.'

'I hope you've got some warm clothes. It's cold this morning, now the rain's gone.' Then he grinned. 'Oh, yes, I forgot. Antarctica.'

I grinned back. 'They made me give all that stuff back. What was left of it. I ruined most of it getting my leg smashed up.'

'Okay, then, I'll let you get on with it.'

I added kindness to the list of my new flat mate's qualities. He'd already proved himself a man of few words and little curiosity. In other words, perfect for me.

Martin left for uni as soon as he had finished fortifying himself with a pile of toast and Vegemite. I was much slower starting my day. I sat for a long time at the kitchen table drinking coffee and watching a flock of little birds busy among the weeds in Martin's back yard. I was beginning to have second thoughts about visiting Colin's father. Nice chap he might be but I wondered what kind of reception I would get from him when he found out who I was. But my mobile phone lay on the table and taunted me until I summoned the courage to ring the number Professor McRae had given me the day before.

Colin's parents lived in Tarragindi and it took me three buses to get there. Plenty of time to chicken out and go home. But finally I arrived at the top of Colin's street and walked down the hill through the sharp black shadows of early afternoon. At the bottom of the hill the street looped around a patch of grass, deep in shade, before rising again into the sunlight. Colin's house was third from the bottom. A police car was parked on the wide grass verge and the front door was open. I was half way up the cracked concrete path when a man came out of the house. He was wearing brown carpet slippers. An ancient dog with a grey muzzle tottered after him.

'Excuse me, are you Mr Wilson?'

'Yes, young lady, what can I do for you?'

His voice sounded weary as if he had been dealing with people for too long.

'I'm Zoe Carter from Brightsward. I called you a couple of hours ago. Is it a bad time? I can come back.'

'No, no, it's fine. The police are here finger-printing. We had a break-in the other day. Come on in and have a cup of tea.'

Mr Wilson ushered me through the door into a room in which the heady perfume from a bunch of huge white lilies was waging a desperate war against the deep-seated smell of old dog. A broken window patched with cardboard. An empty entertainment cabinet, scattered with white powder. The sound of cheerful voices coming from a dark corridor that must lead to the bedrooms. I followed Mr Wilson into the kitchen and sat at a table covered with an ugly plastic cloth while he filled the kettle at the tap.

'I'm afraid you'll have to manage with my company, Miss Carter. My wife is having a lie down and I don't want to disturb her.' Mugs on a tray, a flower-patterned jug filled with milk from the fridge. 'She's taking it very hard, you see. It's been too much for her on top of everything else'

'The robbery?'

He nodded. 'All Colin's photos were on his computer, you see. All his pictures from Casey Station.' Boiling water into a brown tea pot. Patchwork tea cosy from a drawer. 'I've been meaning to get them turned into prints. She asked me often enough.'

'They took his computer?'

He shrugged unhappily. 'TV, video, I didn't care about them. But Colin's computer … it was all we had left. Come through, Miss Carter.'

I stood up and followed Mr Wilson into the front room. He put the tray down on a low table and indicated a slippery leather couch. 'Sit down.'

I sat. 'What about Colin's data? Was that on his computer, too?'

Mr Wilson looked up quickly. 'Is that what you came here for?'

It occurred to me that, underneath his mild expression, Mr Wilson could be a dangerous man. An ex-cop, Professor McRae said he was.

I shook my head. 'I don't want it, Mr Wilson. It's for Professor McRae.'

'Ah, yes, Colin's supervisor. I met him at the memorial service. Gingery little chap.' He nodded towards the lilies. 'That other young girl. The one who brought the flowers. She was after Colin's data too. She said she was from the institute that funded his research. I told her I didn't have it, which was a lie because he'd emailed it to me, every bit, and it was all stored on the computer. I didn't like the look of her, to be honest. A nasty piece of work if ever I saw one.'

'But it's gone now.'

'We'll have to see what we can do.' Mr Wilson poured the tea and handed a mug across to me. 'So how did you meet my son, Miss Carter?'

'I met him at Mawson base on Midsummer Eve. He told me about playing cricket at the bottom of the street.'

'Yes, he told us about you. You're from Bowen, aren't you?'

'Yes, that's me.'

'And you're the one who took him joy-riding in the helicopter?'

'Yes.' I hesitated. 'Mr Wilson …'

But he interrupted me. 'Miss Carter, don't think I blame you for what happened to Colin because I don't. And don't think I haven't read the coroner's report because I have. Every last word. In fact I was in court the day it was handed down.'

'Pilot error,' I said, the words bitter in my mouth.

'Yes, you got the blame fair and square. No doubt about it.' Mr Wilson leaned forward and placed his mug carefully on the table on front of him. 'But tell me this, young lady. Would you be sitting in that chair if you were responsible for my son's death?'

Startled, I stared across the space between us. 'No, of course not.'

Mr Wilson picked up his mug and sipped carefully. 'So why don't you tell me what really happened?'

But I didn't have the chance.

'Ken? You didn't tell me we had a visitor.'

A woman had emerged from the dark corridor. She was neatly dressed and would have been attractive if it were not for the misery etched on her face like a mask. There was no doubt who she was. In his face and his build, even in the way he held himself, Colin had been every bit his mother's son.

'I thought you were lying down.'

Mr Wilson placed his hands on the arms of his chair and stood up slowly, as if every bone ached. He turned his head and sent me a brief, urgent glance that said as clearly as if he had spoken the words aloud – don't let her know who you are.

'Aren't you going to introduce us?' Mrs Wilson bent down to fondle the ears of the old dog that had tottered over to greet her. 'Colin's dog,' she explained. 'He's a bit lost without him.'

'This is Zoe Carter,' said Mr Wilson. ' She's …'

He cast me an imploring glance. He was obviously no better at lying than I was.

'I was a friend of Colin's,' I supplied. 'From uni. I only just found out what happened and I wanted to say how sorry I was.' I stood up. 'I've got to go now. I've got a bus to catch.' I glanced over at Mr Wilson. 'Thanks for the tea.'

'Thank you for coming to see us. I'll see you out.'

He moved towards the door and his hand was on the latch, ready to open it, when a pair of young constables came into the living room.

'All done,' said one. 'We'll get out of your way now.'

'Just a moment, young fellow.' Mr Wilson turned to me and gave me his soft sweaty hand to shake. 'Thanks again for the visit.' He put his hand into his trouser pocket and pulled out a memory stick. 'I've got this for you. It's Colin's data. Please give it to Professor McRae with my compliments.' Then he reached out and opened the door.

'Of course. I'll go tomorrow. Thanks, Mr Wilson.' I was outside the door in the sweet afternoon air but I turned back. 'You should get rid of them,' I said in a sudden passion. 'Those flowers. They stink. Why don't you throw them away?'

Mr Wilson nodded. 'You're right. I'll do it now.'

I don't often cry but I had a knot of tears in my throat as the bus carried me home through the afternoon light. Not just for Colin but for his mother with her mask of grief, and the old dog who didn't know where his master had gone. What I needed to do was to lose myself in Martin's arms and cry against his chest. But he had made no move towards me and I was unsure of how he would react. And this time with this man, I needed to get it right.

SIX

By the time I got home it was almost dark and the wind
from the river had turned cold. I hurried down the path
and put my hand out to open the screen door. But it was no
longer in its place Instead it was lying drunkenly in the dark
evergreen bush that grew up against the wall of the house.
And the front door was shut tight. Shivering in the cold air,
I banged hard with my knuckles.

'Martin. Martin? Come on, open up. I'm freezing out here.'

After a moment the door was yanked open. Martin did not
look pleased to see me.

'What's going on?' I walked around him into the house.

'What does it look like? The screen door's buggered. I gave
it a push and it fell off its hinges.' Martin forced the front
door shut. 'And I can't find a key for this door. I don't think
it's been locked since I moved in.'

In the kitchen the cutlery drawer was upended on the
table. Knives and forks, and an odd assortment of teaspoons.
Bottle tops, old pizza vouchers, sauce sachets. No keys.

I reached for the half-finished bottle of wine on top of the
fridge. 'So how come you wrecked the screen door?'

'I was trying to get to the library,' he said peevishly. 'I'd
already missed one bus because of your friend.'

'What friend?'

He reached out and took his glass of wine from my hand.
'Some girl. She turned up about an hour ago. Said she was a
friend of yours. From Bowen.'

I shook my head. 'I don't have any friends in Bowen.
Anyway how would she know where I was?'

'I dunno, Zoe. Maybe she got the address from your sister.'

I nodded. 'Yeah, that'd be right. Zara must have sent someone down here to check up on me.'

Martin took a gulp of his wine. 'Older sisters, eh?'

'No, she's younger than me. But she always behaves like she's the mature one and I'm some little kid that needs looking after.' I sloshed some more wine into my glass. 'So what did she say, this so-called friend of mine?'

Martin shrugged. 'She didn't say anything.'

'Come on, Martin. She must have said something.'

Martin shook his head. 'She just asked if you lived here and when I said you were out, she just left. No message, no nothing.'

'That's weird.' I reached over and upended the bottle into Martin's glass. 'Look, Martin, I'll get someone to fix the door in the morning if you'll do something for me.' I took the memory stick out of my pocket. 'Can you give this to Colin's supervisor? Professor McRae, in that building down by the river.'

Martin reached out and took the tiny device out of my hand. 'What is it?'

'It's Colin's research data. I got it from his dad.'

'No worries.' He shoved the memory stick in his pocket, then turned to the table and began tossing everything back into the drawer. 'What do you fancy for dinner?'

I grinned. 'Lamb?'

I spent the following morning sitting at the kitchen table drinking coffee while a man called Des, sent by the landlord's agents, fitted a dead lock to the front door. At lunch time Des, having called me 'little lady' once too often, went whistling on his way.

I was left to wonder whether Martin would remember to buy a loaf of bread on his way home and to wish he embraced the modern world enough to have a mobile phone so I could call and remind him. Five minutes later I heard his voice outside the front door.

'Hey, Zoe, come and let me in.'

He was standing on the front path with a tall, good-looking boy with spiky blond-tipped hair. Under his arm was a large, paper-wrapped parcel from which emerged the alluring aroma of hot fish and chips.

'Zoe, this is Jamie. Jamie, my flat mate Zoe Carter.'

'How're you doing, Zoe?' He turned to Martin. 'Is this the door you wrecked? You did a pretty good job.'

Martin shrugged. 'I don't know my own strength.'

Jamie grinned. 'You never did. Remember at school when you sat on that chair?' He turned back at me. 'We were at school together. Haven't seen him since Year 12.' And then, to Martin, 'Look, man, you broke off a whole branch.' He indicated a bunch of dead, dry leaves clustered around the door handle.

'Never mind about that,' said Martin. 'Come inside and let's eat this lot before it gets cold.'

We went into the kitchen and opened up the parcel. There was silence while we ate the fragrant, greasy food. When our plates were empty, Martin got up and filled the kettle at the tap.

'How long before you're allowed back in the lab?' he asked Jamie. 'Jamie works in Professor McRae's lab,' he said to me. 'I met him when I went to drop off your memory stick.'

'What did Professor McRae say?'

A glance exchanged between the two. Martin fumbled in his pocket, pulled out the memory stick and dropped it on the bench.

'He didn't say anything. Professor McRae's dead, Zoe.'

'*Dead?*'

'Heart attack,' said Jamie. 'Only the old fucker had to die in his office, didn't he? So now we're locked out of the lab while the cops sniff around. A pity because I had some work I wanted to get done today.'

'You ... you don't sound very upset.'

'I'll have to find another supervisor but that won't be too hard. He was never much help anyway. Always in his office with the door closed.'

'But he was an expert, wasn't he?' said Martin. He dumped the mugs of tea on the table and turned to the fridge for milk.

'Oh, yes, he was an expert all right. An expert at getting his name on academic papers. That's all he really cared about.'

'What kind of research was he doing?' Martin was leaning against the kitchen bench, his bulk blocking the light from the window.

'He was working on arboviruses. That's what I'm studying for my PhD. A bit more use than Alexander the fucken Great.'

Martin grinned at me. 'Jamie's a scientist. Thinks the world should revolve around him.'

'Too right it should.'

'What's an arbovirus?' I asked. 'It sounds like some sort of tree disease.'

'AR ... BO. Arthropod borne. An arthropod's an insect. So we're looking at diseases carried by insects.'

'Like malaria?'

'Yeah, malaria. Japanese encephalitis, Dengue fever. And Ross River and Barmah Forest viruses which are endemic here in eastern Australia.'

'I've heard of Ross River,' I said. 'A girl at school had it. It's a type of arthritis isn't it?'

Jamie nodded. 'Polyarthritis, they call it. Professor McRae got some money from the World Health Organisation to develop a diagnostic test for Ross River. The problem is that only a quarter of the people infected with the virus develop symptoms, so it's important to be able to test the whole population.'

'Why is that a problem?' asked Martin. 'It doesn't sound like one to me, especially for the people who get the disease but don't get sick.'

'It's a problem because it creates a latent pool of active virus in the population. So it maximises the spread of the disease.'

'And it's carried by mosquitoes?'

'Yes.'

'Person to person?'

'No, there's a marsupial host as well'

'So it goes from a person to a marsupial to a person?'

'Yeah, that's right.'

'And there's no cure?' I asked. 'Or prevention?'

'No, but there should be. The problem is Australia has such a low population by world standards and there are even less people living up here in Queensland where Ross River is most prevalent. Pharmaceutical companies aren't interested in putting money into finding a cure. There simply isn't a big enough market.'

'But what about something like malaria? That affects millions of people, surely?'

Jamie nodded. 'World's biggest killer, bar none. But it's the same deal. Malaria is a disease of the tropics which means most of the people who are affected by it are in the Third World where people can't afford expensive new drugs. So why would pharmaceutical companies spend billions of dollars developing a drug nobody's gonna buy?'

'So the only people doing research into these … arboviruses are academics like you and Professor McRae?'

Jamie nodded. 'Yeah, pretty much at the moment. But things are changing now global warming's beginning to kick in.'

'Why's that?'

'Well, you know, everywhere's gonna get hotter. So tropical diseases will move north into the US and parts of Europe. That's when pharmaceutical companies will begin to make big money. It's perfect timing for me. With a bit of luck I'll be able to cash in big time.' Jamie stood up. 'Anyway I'd better be off. Hopefully I can get back into the lab this arvo so I can do some work on my mozzies.'

'What are you going to do with them?' asked Martin

Jamie grinned. 'Crush 'em with a mortar and pestle.'

'Crush them? What for?'

'Somebody's got to do it. No, it's to extract viral antibodies. Look for the disease,' he explained. 'They're special mozzies shipped from north Queensland.'

Martin pushed himself away from the bench. 'Come on, then. I'll show you out.'

'See you, Zoe.'

'Yeah, see you.'

When they were gone from the kitchen, I went over to the bench and picked up the memory stick. I opened the drawer and dropped it in. Then I stood for a long moment with my hands flat on the kitchen bench to stop them trembling.

'What's going on?'

Martin had come back into the kitchen and was standing behind me. I pushed the drawer shut and turned to face him.

'What do you mean?'

'I saw your face when you heard about Professor McRae. You looked like you'd lost your best mate, not some old bloke you'd only just met.' He reached out and put his hands on my shoulders. 'And Colin. He isn't in the Antarctic, is he? He's dead. Jamie told me.'

'In a sense he is.' I laughed shakily. 'They never recovered his body.'

'Jamie said he died in a helicopter crash.'

'He did. He was my passenger.'

There was silence for a heart beat. Then, 'Do you want to talk about it?' Martin's voice was very gentle.

I shook my head. 'No, not really. Look, Martin, there's more to this than you know. Remember the day we met? It was all bullshit, what I told you. I'm not in Brisbane researching a paper on global warming. Colin was murdered. Someone shot my helicopter out of the sky.' I touched my leg. 'That's how I got this. Since then two other people have died. Dr Maddern in Bowen and, now, Professor McRae. And I think there's a connection.'

'With Colin's death?'

'Yes. And with me.'

'I think we'd better go and sit down.' Martin reached into the fridge for a packet of chocolate biscuits. He was beginning to know my habits.

'Do you know why Colin was murdered?' Martin asked when we were sitting on the old couch in the front room.

'Dr Maddern thought it had something to do with his research.'

'You talked to Dr Maddern about Colin's murder?'

'Dr Maddern was the one who told me about it. Before that I thought the helicopter crash was my fault.'

'And then he was killed?'

'Yes, in a hit and run.'

'So it could have been an accident?'

'It could have been. But now I don't think it was.'

'So why do you think Dr Maddern was killed?'

'Maybe because he knew my helicopter had been shot down. Someone went to a lot of trouble to make that crash look like an accident. If it wasn't for what Dr Maddern saw on my x-ray, nobody would have been any the wiser. Including me.'

Martin reached out his foot and pulled the coffee table closer. He broke open the packet of biscuits and handed one to me. 'So who else knew about it?'

'My sister did. Oh, and Annie Cormack, the girl from Brightsward.'

'Nobody else?'

I thought for a moment. 'Probably my brother-in-law as well because Zara would have told him about it. Hang on a minute ....' I leaned forward and stared down at the stained carpet. Then, 'Listen to this, Martin. Dr Maddern was killed in a hit and run. Next thing, my brother-in-law is at the cop shop explaining why his car has a big ding in the side. Done on the same night.'

Martin raised an eye brow. Said nothing.

'He said he'd hit a 'roo. But I dunno, Martin. What if it was him who killed Dr Maddern?'

'Deliberately?'

'Yes.'

'Because he's involved in Colin's murder?'

'Yes. Well, no. But if someone recruited him … paid him money …'

'Would he do it?'

'I reckon he'd do anything if you offered him enough cash.'

'You don't like him very much, do you?'

'I don't like him at all. But that's not the point.' I hooked one leg underneath my body and turned round to face Martin full on. 'Derek's got some sort of crap job with the local council and they've got two kids and a mortgage. They must be in a heap of debt. And he's always on the Internet. Who knows who he meets in those chat rooms of his?'

'He hasn't been charged, has he? For the hit and run?'

'No, he hasn't. But he was up to something that night, I know he was.'

'Okay, let's leave him for a moment. What about Professor McRae?'

But I didn't answer straight away. As much as I disliked him, the thought of my brother-in-law as some sort of paid killer was freaking me out. Maybe I'd blown the whole thing out of proportion. Made connections where there really weren't any. Only my lurid imagination running wild.

Finally I said, 'I dunno, Martin. Maybe Professor McRae died of a heart attack like Jamie said.'

'Maybe he did. But I saw your face when you found out he was dead. You didn't think it was a heart attack then, did you?' He reached out and grabbed my hands. 'Come on, Zoe, don't give up now! It's always difficult when you're trying to come up with a hypothesis.'

'Come up with a what?'

A quick look to see if Martin was taking the piss. But his face revealed nothing but his usual earnest concentration, his dark eyes staring straight into mine.

'A theory then, call it that. This is how academics do their research, Zoe. Come up with a hypothesis and then try to hang some facts on it.'

'You'd think it would be the other way round. Facts first, theory later.'

'No, you have to have the idea as a starting point. In this case, the starting point is three deaths you think are linked to you, right?

'I suppose so.'

'Okay, so why did Professor McRae die? Hypothetically.'

'Not for Colin's research data because he didn't have it.'

'Yes, but the killer might not have known that.'

'No, that's true.' I didn't speak for a while, turning ideas over and over inside my head. Then, 'It's like someone is trying to wipe Colin's research off the face of the earth. I'll tell you something else as well. Colin's parents' house was broken into the other day and they stole his computer. If Mr Wilson hadn't backed up the data onto that memory stick, it would all be lost.'

'It must be hot stuff if someone is going to such lengths to suppress it. I'd like to think people would kill each other for what I'm doing.'

I grinned. 'You should have been a scientist. Like Jamie.'

'Yeah, right.' Martin stood up. 'I need another cup of tea. D'you want one?'

'Yes, please.' I stood up and followed him into the kitchen.

Martin filled the kettle at the tap and plugged it in. 'Okay, try this. Colin makes some sort of discovery down there in the Antarctic. Something to do with global warming. Something with the potential to make someone a lot of money.'

'Like what?'

'How about that stuff Jamie was talking about this afternoon?' Martin upended two mugs from the draining board and reached into the cupboard for tea bags. 'What if a pharmaceutical company was thinking about investing big bucks into malaria research? They'd need accurate data about global warming, wouldn't they?'

'But everyone knows global warming's going to happen, Martin. Where's the big secret in that?'

'Yes, but maybe this is more about *when* it's going to happen. When will temperatures start to rise? When will malarial mosquitoes move into the temperate zones? Because nobody's going to make any money from new drugs until tropical diseases move into Europe and the US, right?'

I nodded. 'They'd want to be sure their drug was the first on the market.'

'Yes, so Colin's discovery could give them a big advantage.'

'That makes sense. So they kill Colin to shut him up. And then they kill Dr Maddern because he knows about my leg.'

'Yes, because they don't want anybody to find out Colin was murdered.' Martin poured boiling water into the mugs and opened the fridge door for milk. 'And then Professor McRae has his so-called heart attack because they think he'll publish Colin's findings.'

I picked up my mug of hot tea. Cradled it in my hands, feeling the warm steam against my face. 'So, according to this theory of yours, anyone who knows about Colin's research, or his murder, is likely to be a target?'

'Well, yes, that's what it looks like to me.'

I looked up. 'In that case I should be dead, too.'

Martin opened his eyes wide. 'Yes, you should be. If my hypothesis is correct, you should be dead. Or, at the very least, on somebody's hit list. Oh, no. Don't cry. Come here.'

I took a step forward and felt his arms come around me. I pushed my face into his old jumper and swallowed hard on my tears. He smelled of instant coffee and old books. And warmth. Oh, he was so warm. I felt my body flare into wakefulness, a feeling I had almost forgotten in the long months since I injured my leg.

'Zoe, you're shivering.'

'That's because I'm scared.' I pulled away and looked up into Martin's face. 'I feel like I'm being stalked. Everywhere I go, they go.' I glanced at the drawer where the memory stick lurked among the stolen teaspoons and expired pizza vouchers. 'And now we've got that thing in the kitchen drawer. The one thing they want to destroy. What's going to happen next?'

Martin pulled me close. 'I can think of something.'

And there was the feeling again. Only, this time, not just on my side. I reached up my hand and drew his head down to mine. Then I kissed him long and hard.

'Come on, then.'

You've probably seen it a hundred times on TV. Two people with their lips glued together removing each others' clothes in a mad sexual scramble. It didn't happen quite like that for us. It was a cool day and cold in the house, and we just went straight into Martin's bedroom and dived under his musty doona. And I didn't have to worry about the scars on my leg. Martin's fingers found them, lingered briefly, then moved on to more important matters.

We stayed in bed for the rest of the day. I slept long and deeply, soothed by Martin's reassuring bulk and the sound of his breathing as he turned the pages of his old book. When I woke, I fetched cheese and biscuits, and a bottle of the cheap cleanskin red I was buying by the dozen because I didn't like drinking alone and Martin wouldn't share the dear stuff I could well afford to buy. I don't know whether he really believed the story of my Brightsward fortune.

That night the nightmare returned. But it was different this time. I was at the university and it was dark and empty. Panic gripped my throat as I ran down the narrow paths between the buildings. Somebody was behind me, someone was following me. The pain in my leg flared and throbbed, slowing me down. I knew I was going to die.

I woke with a start. Grey dawn light filtered into the room. Martin stood by the bed, holding a mug of tea. 'Here, have this. I've brought you a couple of pain killers'

I struggled into a sitting position. Martin tipped the white tablets into my hand then sat on the edge of the bed.

'Listen, Zoe, I've got to go home this week end. It's my dad's birthday on Sunday and they want me there to celebrate. I was wondering … do you want to come with me?'

'Come with you to the farm? To meet your family?'

Because I knew by then that Martin's family owned a large sheep station somewhere outside Quilpie in western Queensland. Which explained all those grey lumps of frozen lamb that inhabited his freezer.

Martin pulled a face. 'It won't be very exciting, I'm afraid. I just thought … it would get you out of Brisbane for a couple of days. Away from …

'… the people who are trying to kill me. Don't, Martin. You're freaking me out.' I reached out and gripped his hand. 'But it's your dad's birthday, Martin. Won't I be in the way?'

'Why would you be in the way?'

I thought, because I'm an outsider, an outcast, an alien. Because I don't know how to do happy families. Me and Zara are just about it. Plus my mother who only stays in one place because she can't get up and run.

Martin leaned forward and kissed me on the lips. 'Actually, you'd be doing me a favour. My dad's always asking me if I've met a nice girl. Maybe you'll be able to take his mind off what a failure I am in all the other aspects of my life.'

I opened my eyes wide. 'What do you mean?'

'I'm his only son, Zoe. He must have been delighted when

I came along after all those gels.' He reached behind his head to retie his pony tail. 'But now here I am wasting my time in the city instead of helping him run the farm. The sooner I'm through uni and back in the bush the happier he'll be.'

'Doesn't he like you studying?'

'I don't suppose he'd mind if he thought I was doing something useful. He keeps asking me what I'm going do with it when I've finished but I don't know, Zoe. I'm just doing it, that's all.'

'So now he's going to think you're normal because you're going out with me?' I started to giggle. 'That's the funniest thing I've ever heard.'

'What's so funny about that?'

'An unemployed helicopter pilot with a crook leg and a price on her head? The perfect girlfriend.'

'You'll do,' said Martin, annoyingly. 'You reckon you'll be all right to take the bus? It's about an eleven hour trip.'

'Yeah, I'll be fine.' I looked up. 'Thanks, Martin.'

SEVEN

A country town is a country town and Quilpie was not that different from Bowen, except it was surrounded by bare brown paddocks instead of lush green cane, and the air lacked Bowen's rich humidity blown in from the Coral Sea. Quilpie's air reminded me more of Antarctica where it was so dry you had to touch metal every ten minutes to prevent static electricity building up in your body. A truly hair-raising experience, and a cause for mirth among the old hands, until you got into the habit of doing it.

Martin's middle sister, Claire, was waiting for us when the bus pulled up outside the Post Office. She was a tall, big-boned woman who held herself with an unassuming confidence. There was an awkward moment when she moved in for a kiss and I stuck out my hand, something I'd done ever since I found out how much most men dislike it.

She led the way to a dusty ute parked nose-in to the pub further up the street and, for a hopeful moment, I thought she'd read my mind until she said, 'Hop in, they're waiting for us.' And then, 'You get in the middle, Zoe, because you're the smallest.'

Claire drove quickly out of town along a narrow strip of bitumen across which long black shadows were falling from the lone gum trees standing along the side of the road. As she drove, she carried on a rapid conversation with her brother across the top of my head while I sat between them trying to ignore the insistent jangle of pain from my injured leg.

It was an hour's journey from town to Martin's property. By the time we arrived, the sun was almost gone – a red ball sliding down behind a flat, dry landscape. Martin's mother came out to meet us with dogs at her heels and a small, sleepy child on her hip. The child belonged to Claire and was grumpy that he had been left behind to sleep instead of going for a ride into town with his mother.

We were ushered into a big warm kitchen and became the centre of a happy chattering group of people: sisters, husbands, kids and, finally, Martin's father, George, who came in through the back door just as we were sitting down to dinner. He made me sit next to him at one end of the long table and helped me to an enormous plate of roast lamb and vegetables while the family chatter continued back and forth.

I ate my food and thought of me and Zara hidden for shame in my grandparents' house. My grandmother said we'd ruined her life, that she couldn't hold her head up in town because of us. Nobody ever came to the house, I remember that. Nobody ever came and we never went anywhere. And we thought it was normal because it was all we knew.

After dinner, Martin and I were ushered out onto the veranda where we sat holding hands and listening to the chatter and laughter of the sisters washing up in the kitchen. After a while Claire came out carrying two mugs of tea.

'Go away, Martin,' she said. 'I want to talk to Zoe.'

She sat down in Martin's chair and handed one of the mugs across to me.

'No sugar, that's right, isn't it?'

I nodded and took the mug. Sipped my tea and waited for the interrogation.

'So how long have you known my baby brother?'

'About a week.' Was it really only a week?

She raised her eye brow that could have meant you're a fast worker, but her voice continued the same, warm and friendly.

'How did you meet? Are you a student, too?'

I shook my head. 'I'm his flat mate.'

'More than his flat mate, I'd say.' She reached out her hand and touched my arm. 'Come on, Zoe, I've seen you two together. I don't know how you are managing to keep your hands off each other.'

'That obvious, huh?'

She laughed. 'Don't worry, it'll wear off after a couple of kids. Anyway, good on you. It's what he needs. What he's needed for a long time. Not just the sex but, you know, somebody to be with.'

I buried my nose in my mug. 'Makes a change from Alexander the Great.'

'I wish you luck getting him away from those old books.' Claire finished her tea and leaned forward to put her mug on the worn timber of the veranda. 'Martin tells me you're a country girl?'

I nodded. 'Bowen. But I live in Brisbane now.'

Claire laughed. 'It's okay, Zoe. It's only Dad who doesn't like Martin living in the city.'

As if we'd been talking about him all the time.

My leg woke me early the following morning. No tea and painkillers, and no Martin either. We'd slept separately – me in a narrow iron bed in the spare room at the front of the house, him on a camp stretcher on the veranda just outside my window.

Claire was right about Martin and me. Just then all we wanted to do was to climb inside each others' bodies and stay there, so it was hard to lie on that hard, hammocky mattress and listen to his breathing and the creak of the camp bed so close and yet completely out of reach. Because, despite Claire's forthright encouragement of our relationship, our sleeping arrangements seemed to indicate that anything approaching the intimacy we craved would have to wait until we got home.

I found Martin in the kitchen with his mother.

'Tea in the pot,' she said cheerfully, and returned to frying lamb chops in a black pan.

Martin poured my tea and brought it over to me, his look of anxious concern out of proportion to the fact that I hadn't had tea in bed. I soon found out why.

George came in, rubbing his hands together. 'Ah, Zoe, how are you? Sleep well?' He ladled several of the greasy chops onto a plate and sat down at the table. 'Martin tells me you fly helicopters?'

'George, leave her alone and let her eat her breakfast in peace,' said Martin's mother. She smiled at me. 'He's been full of it ever since he found out. He's always wanted to go up in a helicopter.'

I looked up at George. 'Where are you going to get a 'copter?'

'Our neighbour's got one that he uses for mustering. I've already called him. He's expecting us over there as soon as we've finished our breakfast.'

I felt the fear hit me like a hard slap, nasty and unexpected, followed by a slow drub of excitement. I stood up, my chair clattering behind me on the brick floor. 'Excuse me for a moment.'

I made it to my room and Martin followed, closing the door behind him. He crouched down by the bed and laid his arms on my lap.

'What's up, Zoe? I thought you'd be pleased.'

'I am pleased. But I'm terrified, too.' I leaned forward and wrapped my arms around his head. 'The problem is, I don't know if I can do it any more.'

'The accident wasn't your fault.' Martin got up from the floor and sat next to me on the bed.

'I know it wasn't. I know that. But the helicopter crashed.'

'Maybe you need to ...'

'And don't give me that shit about getting back on a horse, either. Maybe that is what I should do. But, you know, Martin, maybe I'll never fly a helicopter again. The way things are going I probably never will. So facing my fears isn't an option I need to think about, okay?'

Martin stood up. 'I'll tell him no, then.'

I looked up at him and saw what there was to see about my big, beautiful boy friend and his big mouth. It had been a chance for him to show off, to let his dad know he wasn't a failure, just because he wanted to study in the city instead of chasing sheep around a dusty paddock. A chance to give his dad something he couldn't get for himself. Yeah, and fuck, I could fly helicopters, of course I could. Not just fly them either. I was damn good. Good enough for Brightsward to take me to the Antarctic and let me loose on the ice canyons. Not many people had done what I'd done.

'No, tell him yes,' I said getting up from the bed. 'I'll just get dressed. And Martin …?'

'What?' He was already halfway to the door.

'Tell him I want a beer afterwards. A cold one.'

A grin. 'No worries.'

An hour later the ute was bumping up the dusty track towards the next-door property with Martin driving and me, once again, squashed in the middle. George got out to open the last gate and Martin drove around the back of the house and parked outside a big metal shed.

'Here we are,' he said. 'You sure you're okay?'

'Look, I'll do it. I'm not backing out now, no matter how I feel.' I slid across the bench seat and got out of the ute. My leg was aching again.

George came around the house with a short stocky man wearing a creased flannelette shirt and faded jeans slung under an impressive beer gut. He had no problems shaking my hand. Maybe flying helicopters made me into some sort of a man.

'Call me Joe,' he said, wiping his hands on the back of his jeans. 'Right, let's get on with it, shall we?'

If he had any qualms about letting a young girl with a limp take his machine into the sky, he wasn't showing them. George and I watched as Joe and Martin slid open the big doors of the shed. And there was the helicopter sitting on the concrete like a small black wasp.

Joe handed me the keys. 'Here you go, girly. Have fun.'

I took the keys and held them in my hand. I stepped out of the sun into the cool shade of the shed and felt my heart skip once then settle down to a steady beat. By the time I'd reached the 'copter and swung myself up into the cabin, my nerves had evaporated, replaced by excited anticipation. The helicopter was well-worn, the seat moulded uncomfortably into someone else's shape, the paint rubbed off the controls. There was a star-shaped crack low down on the windscreen.

'Shouldn't be flying,' I thought. Then, 'Yeah, try stopping me.'

I slipped the keys into the ignition, gunned the motor and heard the familiar whap, whap as the rotors started to turn. I lifted the 'copter off the concrete and nudged her slowly out of the big doors. Then I dropped her gently onto the grass, leaned over to open the passenger door and grinned at George.

'Come on, then, if you're coming.'

George ducked his head and ran under the rotors. He heaved himself up into the cockpit and fitted his body into the passenger seat. We were thigh to thigh in the narrow space but it bothered me less than it was bothering him. I leaned over and fastened his safety harness, then handed him his ear phones.

'Mike here, see? Just talk normally. You'll soon get used to it.'

I settled my own ear phones on my head and grinned at him. 'Okay?'

He nodded.

I twisted the throttle and felt the helicopter surge into the sky. Between my feet I could see the shed with the heat dazzle rising from the roof and two tiny figures standing by the toy-sized ute. I made some more height, then rolled the helicopter to starboard.

'Let's go and take a look at your place,' I said into George's ear.

We did a couple of loops over George's house, then pottered over to the town where the pub had four big red Xs painted on the roof. I could feel George starting to relax. For me it was easy. Too easy. Compared with the winds and whiteness of the Antarctic, flying over this benign, sunny landscape was like flying in my sleep.

'Don't forget you owe me a beer,' I said. Then, 'Anywhere else you want to go?'

'The property next door to mine.' George was pointing. 'I wouldn't mind having a look over there. It's just changed hands.'

'Who bought it?'

'That's what I'd like to know.'

I turned west and headed towards a line of broken hills. Below I could see my tiny black shadow crawling across the glittering surface of a dam. I felt a smile spread slowly across my face and did nothing to suppress it. Because I'd found it again. The thing I love. The thing I do best. Flying helicopters. Though how I was going to get my backside into a helicopter on a regular basis was still something I needed to work out. I glanced across at George and there was Martin's profile in an older face. Maybe … maybe I should find myself a farmer to marry. Marry a farm boy and fly helicopters every day of my life. I grinned. Not such a bad idea.

'Over there,' said George in my ear.

I dragged my mind back from its daydream. Up ahead the dull uniformity of the ground was slashed by a series of red oblongs, like war paint on a warrior's face. To one side of the red slashes, the homestead crouched in a puddle of shade.

'What's going on?'

By now we were flying over the raw red squares which seemed to be shallow excavations.

'I don't know,' said George.

'They look like foundations.'

'Yes, but for what? Out here.'

We were over the homestead now and a man appeared, stepping from the black shade of the veranda into the stark sunlight. I saw him look up, shading his eyes. Then there was a rifle in his hands, the butt against his shoulder, the barrel raised with expert ease. Pointing at us.

The sound of a shot, muffled by the wind, a jerk as the bullet ripped through the rotors, then the helicopter stalled and fell out of control …

I felt the sweat pour down my spine, felt my guts turn to liquid. Automatically I twisted the throttle and set the machine in a steep roll. The terror climbed into my chest as I heard the rotors falter. I gripped the controls with sweat-slicked hands and watched the low hills spool across the windscreen as we changed direction. When I had the helicopter flying straight, I glanced across at George's white face.

'He had a gun.'

'I know he had a gun. He wasn't going to shoot us.'

I shook my head. 'I wasn't prepared to take the risk.'

The fear was gone now, replaced by anger that someone, some little ant of a man, could scare me so thoroughly that I had almost lost control of my craft.

I landed the helicopter like a butterfly on a leaf, just to prove I could, and we were greeted by the promised cold beer and the smell of onions cooking. Joe had the barbie fired up and was throwing huge slabs of raw meat onto the hot grill. A long trestle table was set with plates, cutlery and bottles of sauce. Martin threw his arm across my shoulders and used me as a leaning post while he lapped up his father's unaccustomed approval. Salads and desserts turned up, nursed in the laps of Martin's sisters. Small children ran about and yelled, high on soft drink and excitement.

Late in the afternoon with the lowering sun casting a bronze glow over the dusty landscape I found myself sitting on a picnic chair with a sleepy child on my lap. The child had been dumped on me by one of the sisters and had done no more than twist its head around to see who I was before settling down with a dirty thumb. By then I was a little spaced out on beer and sunshine, and the aftermath of adrenalin. The sisters were busy bathing children from the babies up and would reach this one soon enough. I wondered idly whether they would carry on, once they were through with the children, and I, too, would be showered and changed and popped into a clean bed. It was an alluring thought.

On Sunday afternoon Martin and I climbed onto the bus for the weary journey back to Brisbane. We could have gone on Monday but George thought doing a PhD was a nine to five job and Martin didn't want to give him any reason to think differently. At home we found a carton of rancid milk on the kitchen bench and my mobile phone where I'd left it on the bedside table. There were several messages from Zara and I phoned her straight away with the dying battery my excuse for cutting her off mid-sentence.

'Where have you been?' she asked plaintively. 'I've been calling you all week end.'

But there was no time for my reply before she plunged on.

'Derek's been arrested. He's been charged with the hit and run that killed Dr Maddern.'

'Are you okay?'

It was all I could think of to say while my thoughts ran round inside my mind like frightened mice. Because I had forgotten - hadn't I? - while I bathed in the warm glow of Martin's family, that my life was in danger. That, according to Martin's theory, someone out there wanted to complete the trilogy of people who knew too much about Colin's death. Dr Maddern. Professor McRae. And me.

'Zoe, are you still there?'

'Yes, I'm here.'

'Can you come up?'

To Bowen? Hardly. I might be better off outside Brisbane just then, but Bowen was not my idea of a safe refuge.

'Zoe … ?'

'Yes, Zara, I'm thinking. Look, the battery's running out on the phone. I'll call you back, okay?'

Martin came in carrying a fresh carton of milk and raised his eyebrows as I cancelled the call.

'Zara wants me to go up to Bowen.'

'Do you want to go?' He opened the fridge and shoved the milk onto an empty shelf.

I didn't have time to answer. The phone was still in my hand while I searched for the charger and it wasn't quite dead because it rang again. I rolled my eyes at Martin and lifted the phone to my ear. But it wasn't Zara, bullying me to give her what she wanted. It was Annie Cormack.

'Hiya, Zoe, how are you doing?'

There was that attractive Irish burr beneath the hard New York vowels that took me straight back to the night on the beach, my senses invaded by the warm black sky and the sound of singing and the smell of pot and wood smoke and whales. Her hard hand gripping my thigh as she tried her luck. But the phone was dying fast and all I got from her were a few disjointed words.

'... New York ... photographic exhibition ... stay with Eric ... tickets ...'

And I said 'Okay, okay,' whenever I got the chance, while a grin spread itself across my face.

'What was all that about?' asked Martin when the connection finally went dead and I tossed the phone onto the bench.

'That was Annie Cormack. Looks like I'm going to New York.'

'New York? What for?'

'Brightsward's having an exhibition of my photographs from Antarctica and they want me there. Special guest, Annie said. How cool is that?'

He handed me a mug of tea. 'Are you sure it's a good idea?'

'Why wouldn't it be a good idea?' I gulped the hot tea. 'You mean because you think it might be dangerous? But I'll be with Annie, and Brightsward. How could anything happen to me there?'

'Antarctica, Bowen, Brisbane. These people get around.' He leaned against the kitchen bench hugging his tea.

But Martin, nobody's going to know I'm in New York. And I'll be staying with Eric. Eric van Eps. In his house. His mansion, I should say.' I laughed excitedly. 'I reckon you'll be in more danger here. Where they think I am.'

He nodded slowly. 'You're probably right.'

I grinned. 'I am right. Annie's putting the tickets in the mail today. I fly out at the end of the week.'

'How long will you be away?'

I shrugged. 'Not long. A week. Why? Are you going to miss me?

Martin put his mug down and reached for me. He pulled me close into his arms. 'Of course I'm going to miss you,' he said into my hair. 'And I'll worry about you, too.'

I laughed up at him. 'You'll be able to get some work done.'

He grinned back. 'Good old Alexander. He's been a bit neglected recently.'

EIGHT

Summer in New York. I stared out of the cab window at the congested streets and the wall-to-wall crowds on the sidewalk. The stink of petrol fumes and hot bitumen flooded the cab through the open window, adding to the smell of synthetic pine and old cigarette smoke that breathed from the cracked upholstery. It was an hour's journey from the airport to the city through a dreary landscape of car lots and cheap housing and I had spent most of it semi-comatose on the back seat. I was dizzy with tiredness and jet lag and I had a cab charge card in my pocket, which had come with my flight tickets, so I didn't really care where I was going or how long it took me to get there. I woke when the cab crossed the Queensboro Bridge and the steel girders flicked a pattern of light and shade across my face. Sitting up, I was instantly and finally impressed as the New York skyline laid itself out like a faded frieze against the hot white sky.

I hadn't expected the van Eps mansion to be in a terrace but the street was wide and lined with trees that cast patches of shade on the sidewalks and against the walls of the tall narrow houses. The driver double parked his cab, processed my card and popped the boot, then waited impatiently while I heaved out my suitcase and dumped it on the sidewalk. I watched until he was out of sight then turned to the flight of steps that led from the sidewalk to the van Eps' front door. The hot afternoon sun melted the city grime that had attached itself to my skin, making me feel gritty and uncomfortable. And not a little apprehensive at presenting myself, dishevelled and travel-worn, to whoever lived behind this imposing façade.

The front door was opened by a grim middle-aged man in a dark suit who admitted me into an imposing hall with a high ceiling, a shiny tiled floor and an ornate staircase with a curved wooden banister. He took the suitcase out of my hand and dumped it on the floor before stalking away to an inner door, leaving me alone just long enough to destroy what little was left of my self-confidence.

'Zoe!'

Annie Cormack came down the wide stairs and crossed the floor to grab my hands. I wondered why I had bothered to buy a whole new wardrobe of clothes because she was wearing a pair of faded denim shorts and a plain white tee shirt. Looking fabulous in them, too, with tanned arms and her spiky red hair tipped with gold. She leaned down and grabbed my case.

'Come on, I'll show you to your room.'

She led the way across the hall to a lift hidden behind an ornate iron grille. The lift ground its way slowly upwards and opened to a wide corridor with a faded carpet and a number of heavy wooden doors, all fast shut. At one end, a tall window allowed the harsh outside light to infiltrate the silent gloom.

'Here we are. It's all ready for you.'

The room was huge, high-ceilinged, with ponderous furniture in a depressing dark wood. Heavy drapes filtered the hot afternoon glare. Through a half-open door I could see a tiled floor covered with a thick white rug, and the corner of a peach-coloured bath tub. Neatly folded white towels lay on the bed. It was like a room in a three-star hotel.

'I thought you'd like to wash up and take a rest. I'll send Celeste up with something to eat. If there's anything else you need, just ask.' Annie was heading out of the door. 'See you at dinner. Seven thirty sharp. No need to dress up.'

After she'd gone, I crossed to the window and pulled back the heavy curtains. The room was at the back of the house and looked out across narrow yards to the back of another row of houses criss-crossed with metal fire escapes. Some mansion, I thought. It was better in Bowen in my grandparents' house, where the bedroom I'd shared with my sister looked out at lush green cane fields and a high, blue sky. It was better in Brisbane where the window in Martin's room peered over tatty shrubs at the wide brown river. Or Martin's parents place surrounded by paddocks as far as the eye could see. All around me I was aware of the sounds of the vast city, muffled by the thick walls of the house. I let the curtain drop back into place. I didn't like being in a place where I couldn't go outside. It freaked me out.

I was showered and dressed in a thick white robe when I heard a knock at the door. A girl came in carrying a tray. A very young girl with black hair and smooth olive skin.

'Good afternoon, madam,' she said shyly. She put the tray down on a little table by the window. 'I am Celeste. Anything you want, you ask.'

'*Gracias*,' I said, trying out the Spanish I'd picked up during my stay in the hospital in Buenos Aires.

'*Ide nada*,' she replied, looking a little startled.

I wasn't particularly hungry after all the odd meals I'd been given on the long flight from Australia but it seemed as if the tray had been prepared by someone who knew exactly what I'd feel like eating. A perfect omelette. A green salad in a pretty painted bowl. A dish of fresh strawberries. After I'd eaten, I lay on the bed and willed my eyes to close. Through the wall came the muffled thud of music. I wondered if it was coming from Madeleine's room. Madeleine, Eric van Eps' doped-out grand-daughter who Annie credited with saving the world single handed just by her very existence. I was looking forward to meeting her.

I woke with a crash. I was flat out on the bed. Two tall windows revealed a muted evening light. I had no idea where I was. A tap at the door.

'Madam?'

It was Celeste. And I remembered. New York. The heavy, impersonal room. The murmur of the city beyond the sealed windows. I felt the dizzy jet lag reassert itself in my brain.

The door opened a crack. 'Madam, you must hurry. Dinner in five minutes.'

'What time is it?

'Nearly half past seven. *Prisa!*'

I rolled my legs off the bed. 'Okay. Give me a couple of minutes.'

'I wait by the lift.'

Obviously Celeste had been instructed to produce me *pronto*, if not before. It seemed that Eric van Eps ran a tight ship. But, then, when I met him, I wasn't so sure.

I dressed quickly in a crumpled skirt and a clean tee-shirt, then hurried downstairs and through the door held open for me by the anxious little maid. Inside, a long dining table was set for five. Four people were in their seats, all staring towards the door. At the head of the table was Eric van Eps. He looked older than the photograph that was used on all Brightsward's promotional material. A big, solid man all the same. Coarse brown hair streaked with grey. Those alive, alert eyes that spoke to you from the video, or the poster, or the pamphlet. That made you want to do stuff. But he looked tired. Ill. His pale skin had the texture of soft cheese going off.

He stood up. 'Zoe! Welcome.' His voice had the clipped accents of a Dutchman.

I walked around the table and took his proffered hand. 'I'm sorry I'm late.'

'Ach, jet lag. It happens to us all. Now you know Annie, of course, and Nicole, too, *ja?*'

I turned to the girl sitting next to Annie. Nicole had been the expedition leader on the *Astral Traveller*. I hadn't seen her since the hospital in Buenos Aires.

I grinned. 'Hiya, Nicole.'

'Hi, Zoe. I'm glad to see you're up and about. How's the leg now?'

'Much better, thanks.'

'And the photos are great! We're going to have a slide show after dinner. We want to make a final selection of the ones that'll go in the exhibition. I hope you can make it?'

'Yeah, sure. No worries.'

Which left the young girl sitting on Eric's other side.

'And this is my grand-daughter, Madeleine. She's been looking forward to meeting you.

She was nineteen, maybe twenty. Tall and slender. Her grandfather's slightly gingery hair was translated into a stunning auburn which was combined with the flawless, creamy skin of the very young. She was dressed in a neat, collared blouse but I thought the low-cut top Nicole was wearing which was exposing a bit too much of her scraggy neckline would have looked wonderful on this girl.

I sat down in the seat next to Madeleine and smiled at her. 'I'm glad to meet you. Are you in the room next to mine?'

Her eyes looked a question.

'The music. I heard music, that's all. I thought it might have been yours.' It seemed as if I was explaining to the whole table.

Madeleine lowered her gaze. 'I'm sorry if I disturbed you.'

'No, it's okay. It's fine. Don't worry about it.'

Dinner was served by Celeste and the man who'd opened the front door to me earlier that day. The food was as delicious as my lunch had been. I noticed that Eric ate very little of his steamed fish that took the place of our rich Moroccan chicken and fragrant couscous. Once or twice I saw him grip his stomach and grimace with pain. One time he caught my eye and grinned apologetically.

'I have some stomach trouble,' he said 'Old age is a cruel thing.'

At the end of the meal Annie handed him a small glass containing a chalky mixture which he downed in one gulp. Then he gripped his stomach again. 'I think I'll go upstairs. No, no, I can manage.' He waved his hand impatiently as Annie moved to help him to his feet. 'Show me the photos in the morning. Good night, Zoe. We'll talk tomorrow, *ja*?'

It was nearly midnight when I got back to my room. My eyes were gritty with tiredness. My leg was a red ball of pain. The bed had been turned down but it didn't invite me. What did was the faint aura of pot smoke coming from the window where the summer darkness throbbed with the city's lights. I remembered what I'd said to Dr Maddern that night on the beach front in Bowen. The night before he was killed. As a painkiller, marijuana was second to none. Plus, it made you feel good and, just then, I desperately needed something to make me feel better about being in such a lonely, alien place.

I fumbled with the catch and finally pushed up the heavy sash window. Cool night air poured into the room, releasing the smell of dust and mothballs from the thick curtains. Madeleine was sitting on the fire escape with her feet dangling over the edge. She turned her head and I saw a mask of fear drop over her face.

I grinned and held out my hand. 'Toke me up?'

The fear fell away from her face. She reached up and handed me the half-smoked joint. I took a greedy gulp. 'Thanks.'

'Come on out,' she said, shifting herself to make room on the metal platform.

'No, I can't. My leg's hurting too much.'

'What's wrong with it?'

'I hurt it when I crashed your grandfather's helicopter.'

'Oh, yeah.' She raised her eyes to my face. 'You must have smashed it up pretty good.'

I took another drag and passed the joint back to her. 'It's okay. Give it a couple of days and it'll settle down.'

We shared the joint between us in peaceful silence. When it was finished she pinched out the flame and put the stub into a small tin. There was silence for a while, then she seemed to make up her mind about something.

'Look,' she said, 'in your room there's a sort of Chinese screen. Black silk with red figures on it?'

I nodded. 'What about it?'

She stood up. 'There's a door behind it that leads into my room. These rooms were the nursery back in the old days when there were children living in the house, that's why there's a connecting door. Come into my room and we can talk. If you want to?'

It was such a charming mixture of command and childish innocence that, despite the fizzy tiredness that was taking control of my brain, I was instantly hooked.

'Yeah, okay. Not for long, though. I'm pretty tired.'

Madeleine's room. The white paint on the walls didn't quite hide the floral wallpaper underneath. The canopy bed was hung with sheer purple curtains and piled with Indian cushions and soft toys. More of the purple curtains at the windows, fluttering in the cool night air. Posters on the wall. Frogs. Tigers. A waterfall hung with a bright rainbow. Luminous stars were stuck on the ceiling in a pattern I didn't recognise. There was a bunch of candles flickering on the dressing table. The effect was of a little girl's room that an older girl hadn't quite managed to disguise. And maybe didn't want to.

'Do you like it?' Madeleine was throwing cushions off the bed onto the floor.

Yeah, it's great. A bit different from my room.'

'Yes, well, yours is the guest room, isn't it? And we don't have that many visitors.'

I indicated the cushions. 'I don't think I can sit on the floor, Madeleine. Not tonight.'

'Sorry. On the bed, then.'

I climbed onto the bed and lay back among the teddies.

'What about Nicole? Have I kicked her out of the guest room?'

'No, she's gone home. I heard Johannes order a car.'

'Johannes? Is he the bloke who served at dinner?'

Madeleine nodded. 'He takes care of my grandfather.'

'He looks like a bit of a thug.'

Madeleine grinned. 'He *is* a thug. I wouldn't mess with him, if I were you.'

'And Annie? Has she gone home, too?'

Oh, no, Annie lives here. She's got a room downstairs next to the office'

Madeleine climbed off the bed and prowled around the room. She came back with a bag of lollies which she tore open with her teeth.

'How come?' I dipped my hand in the bag.

Madeleine shrugged. 'She says she likes to work late.'

'No, I mean how come she lives here?'

Another shrug. 'I dunno. She moved in when she was between apartments and she's never left. I guess it's good for Opa to have her here just now. She's doing a lot of work for Brightsward while he's ill.'

'What's wrong with him?'

'It's his stomach. Nobody can tell him what's wrong with it. He's been to every kind of doctor but the tests keep coming up negative.' She pulled another lolly out of the bag and crammed it into her mouth. 'They just say do less, take a break but he's doing less now than he's ever done and it just keeps getting worse and worse.'

'What about you? Do you work for Brightsward, too?'

Madeleine laughed. 'I'm its pin-up girl, didn't you know? The reason Brightsward exists.'

'Yeah, I've heard.'

Madeleine turned her head. Her eyes were black in the pale oval of her face.

'But you know what I want to do? I want to live in *this* world. I want to go out. Have fun. You know?'

Well, I didn't know, not really. Fun had never really figured in my life. First I'd lived in Bowen. Then I'd worked for Brightsward. Now I was here with my leg setting up a persistent shriek of pain that I wasn't going to be able to ignore for much longer. And she sounded so much like your typical poor little rich girl that I was tempted to give her a sharp answer. The sort of thing I could imagine Annie saying. Or Martin's sister, Claire. But the look on her face didn't match the whine in her voice. Madeleine van Eps was unhappy. Genuinely unhappy. I knew the symptoms only too well.

From: Zoe Carter [zoecarter@brightsward.com]
To: m.christian@uni.edu.au
Cc:
Subject: Hiya

Sunday arvo and I've finally got time to send you an email. Now I'm sitting in front of the computer I don't know what to say. I really miss you. And I am so far away I can't imagine where you are or what you are doing. The exhibition is going to open on Wednesday evening so I should be out of here by next week end. We have chosen the photos and the graphic artist is busy colour-balancing the images. Already they look a little bit weird and unreal.

Not like the photos I remember taking, that's for sure.

I've been to Brightsward headquarters, it's a very modern shop in an old building in downtown New York. I always thought 'downtown' meant the suburbs but Brightsward are right in the middle of the city, just off Times Square. It must cost them a fortune! We're not sure if Eric will be able to come to the opening. He's pretty sick at the moment so it's good that Annie can take over for him. It seems like she pretty much runs the show anyway.

I've spent a fair bit of time with Eric's granddaughter, Madeleine. She's a nice girl but she doesn't seem to know what she wants to do with her life. It doesn't help that her grandfather gives her no freedom at all. It's got something to do with her mother, apparently, but I don't know what. Consequently she spends a lot of her time on the fire escape smoking pot. Not sure where she gets it, I don't suppose it comes in with the groceries!

I'll let you know when I'm flying back so you can stock up on wine and chocolate.

Zoe.

It's a funny thing but on Sunday night after I'd sent the email to Martin I found out that Madeleine's pot did indeed come in with the groceries. Madeleine and I were on the fire escape in what had become a nightly ritual. I was able to climb over the window sill by now because my leg had finally forgiven me for all the terrible things I'd done to it on the flight over and had subsided to its usual dull throb. It was a hot, oppressive night. The sky was lit from underneath by the lurid yellow glow of the city. The only stars in sight were those that gleamed a weird green on Madeleine's bedroom ceiling.

I wasn't smoking. It wasn't an everyday thing for me any more, now that my pain was under control, and I didn't want to use up Madeleine's stash without being able to replace it.

'Don't worry about that,' she said. 'I can get as much stuff as I want.'

She was leaning on the metal railing streaming smoke away from the house although I didn't know why she bothered. She'd already told me there was nobody at the back of the house except the two of us. Eric had a suite of rooms at the front and his man, Johannes, also slept at the front of the house in a room on the other side of the lift from my own.

'I always wanted to have Opa's room when I was a little girl,' she'd said. 'There's a secret staircase in there, see, hidden behind one of the panels.'

'A secret staircase?' I was intrigued. 'What's it doing there?'

She laughed. 'They're fire stairs really but I used to love them when I was a kid. I could run all over the house and nobody knew where I was.'

'Where do they go?'

'Down to the room next to the office, but that's Annie's bedroom now.' She pulled a face. 'And up to the roof.'

'The roof? What's up there?'

'Opa's helicopter.'

'There's a helicopter up there?'

'Sure there is. But Opa hasn't used it since he got sick.'

'No good offering my services as a pilot, then,' I'd said.

But just knowing that helicopter was up there on the roof allowed me to imagine myself flying again, once I'd managed to clear my name. Flying and Brightsward - they were the only things I really cared about. Except now there was Martin, too.

Now I said, 'So where do you get it from? Your stash?'

'Dimitri, the grocery boy, brings it. He's got a key to the kitchen.' She grinned. 'He's kinda cute. If you like small, dark boys. Doesn't sound like you do.'

Madeleine had listened to me going on about Martin enough to know my current taste in men. I guess it sounded like I was in the middle of some great love affair which wasn't my normal style at all. I was more of a love 'em and leave 'em type of girl but there was something about Martin that was different from my usual run of boy friends. A keeper, my grandmother might have called him. The sort of boy you marry. Which, strangely enough, was a thought I actually quite liked.

I watched Madeleine take another gulp of smoke. 'You shouldn't smoke every day, you know, Madeleine. It'll do your head in.'

'What else am I supposed to do?'

'Well, if you didn't do so much stuff, maybe you'd be able to think of something.'

She shook her head. 'You don't know what's going on in this house, Zoe.'

'What *is* going on?'

She shrugged. 'I dunno. But something is.'

'To do with you?'

'Well yeah, I guess. And don't say I should do something about it because I can't.' She pushed herself away from the railing and sat down on the step next to me. 'There's going to be a storm tonight.'

I looked up at the patch of sky over the opposite house. 'How do you know?'

'I can feel it.'

I turned and stared at her. 'Feel it? How can you feel a storm in the middle of New York?'

'I just can. It's hot for a couple of days, then it's like the air is pressing down on your head. Then there's a storm.'

'It's like that in Bowen when a cyclone's brewing.'

'You can smell it now.' Madeleine lifted her head. '

'It's frustrating,' I said. 'Storms are good fun to watch.'

'Not from here.'

'Come to Queensland. I'll show you storms.'

'I'd like that.'

The melancholy was back in Madeleine's eyes.

'Well, do it then.' I stood up. 'I'm going to bed. See you tomorrow.'

Wednesday afternoon and we were in the gallery behind the Brightsward shop. Me, Annie and Nicole, checking on the caterers and making sure the pictures were hanging straight. The thunderstorm had cleared the air and it was a sparkling summer day, visible through the big windows of the store but not felt in the artificial atmosphere inside.

Nicole was dressed in a navy and white suit, ready for the evening. She seemed perfectly comfortable to spend the whole day in clothes that would have suffocated me in five minutes flat. After a while she left on an errand and

Annie beckoned me into the kitchen where the caterers were polishing glasses and setting out trays of canapés.

She opened the fridge and hooked out a bottle of wine, twisted the lid and sloshed wine into two glasses. Then she nudged open the back door, letting in warm, gasoline tainted air. Outside was a hot little yard with a plastic table and a couple of dirty chairs. We sat down. Annie handed me a glass, beaded with moisture.

'I just wanted to talk to you about Madeleine,' she said. 'I think I told you about her before. She's a pot head. No ambition, no drive, no nothing. She's breaking her grandfather's heart. And you're not helping, smoking with her on the fire escape every night.'

I looked up, startled.

'You can smell that stuff a mile off, you should know that.' Annie took a sip of her wine and placed the glass on the table, her blunt fingers caressing the stem. 'Madeleine admires you. Sees you as some kind of role model. So having you out there night after night just reinforces the behaviour in her mind.'

I fought the urge to hang my head. Took refuge instead behind my wine glass. It was like when I was a little kid facing up to my grandmother over something I was supposed to have done.

'Maybe if her grandfather let her off the leash once in a while?'

Annie leaned forward. 'You don't get it, do you? Madeleine's mother died of a heroin overdose. Madeleine was only two years old when it happened. It was just as well Eric managed to find out where she was.'

'Why? Where was she?'

'Living in some apartment down in New Jersey. Her mother had taken up with some druggie years before. I don't think Eric even knew Madeleine existed until it was plastered all over the newspapers.'

'The papers?'

'Eric van Eps' only child dies of a drug overdose? Why wouldn't it be all over the papers?

'So what happened then?'

'Eric brought Madeleine back here. Gave up all his business interests and started Brightsward. You know the rest.'

'So you're telling me Eric keeps Madeleine on a tight rein so she won't end up like her mother? Doesn't seem to be working too well, does it?'

'He loves her. He wants what's best for her. He's *ill*.'

'So you're looking out for her?'

'I'm doing what I can.' Annie drained her glass. 'Just keep away from her, that's all I'm saying. She's bad news. And if you want a future with Brightsward you need to keep your nose clean. With Eric, not me.' She stood up. 'Now, come on, let's go inside and smile for the lovely people.'

NINE

It was easier than I thought to keep away from Madeleine. Wednesday was a late night, Thursday I packed and went to bed early. Friday morning I was out of there. And I was never so glad in my life to get back to Queensland. After all the security checks I'd endured in the US, it was a relief to fly into Brisbane Airport where the only thing they cared about was whether I was carrying food in my baggage. And Martin was waiting for me on the other side of the barrier when I dragged my suitcase through the customs area and out of the exit door.

I slept late the following morning, stupefied with jet lag and sex, and it was almost eleven o'clock when I wandered blearily into the kitchen. Martin had cleared his books off the kitchen table and was absorbed with lots of little squares of red and green cardboard. He looked up when I came in and went to fill the kettle. 'Tea?'

'Yes, please. What's going on here?'

'Battle of Gaugamela. When the boy from Macedonia defeats the emperor Darius and becomes ruler of the Persian empire. Pretty amazing, huh?'

'So is that Alexander's army?' I pointed to the predominant red squares.

'No way,' said Martin. He dropped a couple of pieces of bread in the toaster. 'Those are Darius' forces. Alexander was heavily outnumbered by the Persians. But he was smart. And he led the cavalry charge himself. The Persians had never seen anything like it.'

Martin dumped a mug of tea and a plate of toast at the edge of the battlefield and returned to his cardboard armies.

'What are you going to do today?'

'I'm going to give Mr Wilson a call. I need to go and see him.'

A flicker of interest. 'Why?'

'I was thinking about Colin when I was on my way back from New York.'

'Why were you thinking about him?'

I grinned. 'You're not jealous, are you?'

'Nothing to be jealous about. I'm just curious, that's all.'

I leaned forward and kissed the only bit of Martin I could reach, which was the top of his head because he was still fiddling with his pieces of cardboard.

'I was thinking about him because it was dark, and my leg was aching and we were flying over the date line. And it reminded me of when Brightsward flew me home from the hospital in Buenos Aires. When I thought Colin's death had been my fault. And I started thinking of our hypo ... hypo ...'

'... hypothesis.'

'Yeah, that thing. And it occurred to me that we'd missed something. Something important.'

'What?'

I had his attention now.

'It occurred to me that the people who went to so much trouble to destroy Colin's evidence must have had access to it themselves. Otherwise how would they have known what he'd discovered? And I thought, why not the institute that funded his research?'

'So what's the connection with Mr Wilson?'

'Someone from the institute went to see him. Took him a bunch of stinky flowers. And I thought he might know who they are.'

But I'd lost him. Martin's interest had drifted back to the table.

'Tell you what, Zoe. You go and see Mr Wilson. That's a good idea. And we can talk about it tonight. It's just that I've got to get Alexander's cavalry into the right position ...'

At the top of Mr Wilson's street a strip of shops had

undergone a make-over to cater for the trendy brigade that was taking over the old suburb. Bakery, florist, deli, book shop. Terracotta pots holding green ficus and bougainvillea. Halfway along, a café with tables and chairs spilling out onto the footpath. Mr Wilson was sitting at an empty table, looking out of place in his K-mart slacks and hand-knitted jumper. He stood up when he saw me, almost toppling the flimsy aluminium chair.

'How are you, Miss Carter? I'd offer to buy you a coffee but I don't know what to ask for in these fancy places.'

'It's okay. I'll get them.'

At least New York had been good for something, I thought, as I went into the dark little shop and stared up at the menu board. My grandparents used to buy kilo tins of Pablo that Bowen's humidity turned into thick, black treacle. When I moved out I'd changed to International Roast and thought I was the height of sophistication. And it was a while before I abandoned my tube of condensed milk in favour of the fresh stuff out of a carton. But now, courtesy of Eric's breakfast table, I was ready to die for a double-shot espresso with a dash of cream.

I came out of the shop with my espresso, a flat white for Mr Wilson and a plate of fruit toast because it was now mid-afternoon and lunch had somehow passed me by.

'Here you go.' I put the cup down in front of him.

'Thank you, Miss Carter.'

I sat down opposite him. 'You'd better call me Zoe.'

'Zoe, then.'

I noticed he didn't offer his own name which was just as well. I couldn't imagine calling him anything other than Mr Wilson.

Mr Wilson tore open two tubes of sugar, poured the sugar into his coffee and stirred it in. He picked up the cup between his thumb and forefinger and sipped suspiciously.

Then, 'You're looking for the name of the institute that funded Colin's research. May I ask why?'

I picked up a piece of the fruit toast and shredded it between my fingers. Finally I said, 'Someone shot my helicopter out of the sky. I want to find out who it was.'

'Deliberately?'

'Yes.'

'Do you know why?'

I took a deep breath. 'To kill your son. But I think you know that already.'

Mr Wilson's thick fingers planted his cup in the saucer. 'You know what I was before I retired, Zoe? I was a cop. I did twenty years in the drug squad.' He lifted one finger and tapped the side of his fleshy nose. 'I've got a cop's nose and it doesn't disappear when you give up the job. You know what my nose told me about Colin's death?'

He reached into his trouser pocket for a cotton handkerchief, blew his nose and stuffed the crumpled square back out of sight.

'The whole thing smelled wrong from the start. Colin sends me an email and tells me he's made a major discovery. Watch out world, sort of idea. Next thing I know, he's dead and someone from this institute of yours turns up on my doorstep wanting his data. Now I know, because Colin told me, that he'd sent all his data to the institute, every bit. So I asked myself, why did the institute want his data when they already had it? And why did they want it so badly they sent someone all the way from New York to get it? Because that's where that young lady came from. She told me so herself. Next thing you turned up. I'll tell you something else you learn as a cop. You learn how to read people.' He leaned forward and pointed his big, blunt finger at me. 'You came to my house with something to say and you didn't say it.'

'It was difficult. I … I didn't know how you'd react if I started asking questions. And then Colin's mum interrupted us, remember?'

'Yes, that's right, she did. All the same, I regretted not getting your phone number before you left. If we'd been able to have another conversation maybe you would have told me what was on your mind.'

Well, I regretted it, too. I thought of Martin with his careful academic theory and what Mr Wilson had learned by using his cop's nose. Colin and his data. It all came back to that.

'It doesn't sound like I had much more to tell you than you'd already worked out for yourself.'

'Colin was murdered.'

I nodded. 'We think …'

'We?'

'My boy friend Martin and I. He's a student at the university.'

I didn't mention Alexander the Great. I didn't think Mr Wilson would understand about him.

'Go on.'

'We don't think the person who came to your house wanted Colin's data. We think she wanted to make sure nobody else could get hold of it. That's why she arranged for someone to break in and steal Colin's computer.'

A look that might have been approval. 'She arranged it? I hadn't thought of that. The question is why don't they want anyone else to know about Colin's discovery?'

'We don't really know the answer to that one, Mr Wilson. Maybe because Colin found something they could profit from. And they wanted to get in first.'

Mr Wilson nodded his head. 'Yes, that makes sense. Has Professor McRae had a look at the data yet?'

I shook my head. 'Professor McRae's dead.'

Mr Wilson hoisted an eye brow. 'Dead?'

'Heart attack. Or so they say.'

'So where's the data now?'

'I've got it at home.'

'I hope it's somewhere safe.'

'I shook my head. 'Nobody knows it exists. Except us.'

'Don't be too sure about that.' Mr Wilson pulled a battered leather wallet from his pocket and extracted a square of white cardboard. He handed it across the table to me. 'Here's what you're after.'

A florists' card. Typewritten regrets under a picture of a yellow daisy. And a name: The MMC Research Institute.

I looked up. 'I've never heard of them.'

'Neither have I.' Mr Wilson reached out his big hand and flipped the card over. 'That's their registered address. I looked it up on the Internet.'

Scribbled words in blue pen. '2794 East 47th Street, New York.'

A moment's silence.

Then, 'I know where that is. It's Brightsward's headquarters. I was there last week.' My eyes widened. 'But Brightsward can't be responsible for … for murder?'

'You can't say that for sure.' Mr Wilson leaned forward and planted his finger on the small white card. 'A big organisation like Brightsward. Plenty of room for a bad apple.'

I thought of the people I'd met in New York. The only bad apple I'd come across was Madeleine van Eps and she couldn't even get herself out of bed in the morning, never mind organise murder and theft on another continent half way around the world. Two continents, if you counted Antarctica. And why would she want to? But the question always came back to why.

I sighed. 'I wish I'd had this information a week ago. I could have done some snooping around while I was in New York.'

Mr Wilson placed his big soft hand over mine. 'My dear young lady, if there is a killer in either organisation, snooping around is the last thing you'd want to be doing. Just be glad you're over here and out of the way.'

'So how am I supposed to find out what happened to Colin?'

'Not by putting your own life in danger. Anyway what is it to you why he died? He was *my* son.'

I stared across the table at the big ex-cop. 'Because I need to clear my name.'

'Clear your name?'

'Pilot error. Remember?'

'The inquest. Of course. You want to go back to flying helicopters.'

'What about you? Don't you want to know what happened to him?'

Mr Wilson lifted his hands from the table in an empty gesture. 'He's dead, Zoe. There's nothing anyone can do about that.'

And then there was nothing left to say. We sat for a moment

finishing our coffee then Mr Wilson stood up. 'Good to see you again.' He offered me his hand. 'Keep in touch, all right?'

I wondered briefly if it was a request or an order, but nodded anyway.

'Yeah, okay. And thanks for the information.'

'Glad I could help.'

I watched Mr Wilson escape the crowded café area and shoulder his way along the street. Then I picked up the florists' card and shoved it into my pocket. It was another piece of the puzzle but I had no idea where it fitted in. And it would be a while before I had the head space to work it out. Tomorrow I was flying up to Bowen to visit my sister. And I wasn't looking forward to it.

TEN

I have to say, Zara's house was a much happier place with the arse-hole gone. The computer had been moved from the shed into the living room and the girls were absorbed in a game that involved a lot of noise and giggling. Zara and I took our glasses of wine into the kitchen while she cooked dinner. It seemed Zara had taken over from me as the drinker of the family. I was more into tea these days which Martin absorbed by the bucket load while he battled with his thesis. And it was good wine, too, not the stuff out of a cask she used to keep at the back of the fridge in the good old Derek days.

I have always had an aversion to cask wine and not just because of the taste either, because you can get used to anything if you work hard enough at it. But I have always found something vaguely disturbing about the bit at the end when you drag the bladder through the hole in the cardboard and squeeze it scientifically into your glass. Overtones of gynecological procedures that don't really bear thinking about.

Zara had found herself a part-time job as a teacher aide at Tina's school, the kind of job married women did for pocket money, and I wondered where the money was coming from for the bottles of wine, to say nothing of the plasma TV that had materialised in the corner of her lounge room. Obviously, having her old man banged up in prison hadn't made any difference to Zara's spending habits. But my sister had always been able to find a way to get what she wanted.

After the girls had gone to bed we sat together in the lounge room finishing the second bottle while people got murdered in glorious technicolour on the TV screen in the corner of the room.

'So,' I said, as she poured the last of the wine into my glass, 'when am I going to have the pleasure of visiting my brother-in-law in prison?'

Zara reached for the remote and turned down the sound. 'He isn't in prison, Zoe. They let him out on bail. Running over someone is hardly a crime, you know.'

'So where is he?'

A careless shrug that didn't match the look of irritation that had taken possession of her face.

'He's in a flat somewhere. I wouldn't have him back in the house once I found out what he'd been up to.'

She made him sound like a dog that had eaten something unspeakable. I took a careful sip of wine and watched her over the top of my glass.

'What else did he do, apart from killing Dr Maddern?'

'Not the *accident*, Zoe. What he'd been up to on that computer of his.' She gulped the rest of her wine. 'He'd been meeting women on the Internet. Going onto dating sites and picking up these sluts. He told me he was going out to … to clear his head …'

'But it wasn't his head he was clearing?'

'No.' Zara shook her head fiercely. 'Not it was not.' She looked up at me. 'How could he do such a thing, Zoe? How could he?'

Quite easily, I thought. He'd treated my sister like shit since the day he met her. It was one of the reasons I'd never liked him.

'It explains one thing,' I said. 'You remember the night Dr Maddern was killed? Derek said he'd been down on the beach front getting a breath of fresh air. Well, I was down there myself that night and I didn't see him.'

'That's what he told the police he was doing,' said Zara. 'You were supposed to corroborate his story.'

'No way, Zara. It's like him saying he got home at two am when it was more like four.'

'Well, he got found out in the end. He was bound to, really. Bowen's a small town.'

'So why did he lie to the police? What was the point?'

'He was probably hoping to stay out of trouble at home. Telling the truth to the cops would mean I'd find out what he was really doing.'

'So how did you find out? If it wasn't from him?' I got up and went into the kitchen to put the kettle on. The wine had made me thirsty.

'It was when I decided to move the computer into the house so the girls could use it. I got someone in reconnect it and he found all this stuff on there. All the conversations Derek had with these women' The look of annoyance was back on my sister's face. 'And the porn, Zoe. It was disgusting. Thank God I found it before I let the girls use the computer. The kettle's boiled.'

I went back into the kitchen and made the tea. I brought the mugs in with a packet of chocolate biscuits I'd found in the fridge and dumped them on the coffee table.

'And to think I used to make him a cup of tea every night,' said Zara, leaning forward to pick up her mug, 'and took it down to him in the shed while he was ...'

But I'd stopped listening. Because suddenly, listening to my sister tell this sad and sordid domestic tale, I'd realised my theory – our theory, mine and Martin's – had fallen into a great big steaming heap. My brother-in-law a hired assassin working for a shadowy research institute? Yeah, right. Faced with the truth about Derek's grubby little secret, the idea that he had killed Dr Maddern to shut him up about Colin's death was quite simply ridiculous.

The next morning Zara took me to the nursing home on her way to school. Mum seemed to have shrunk since the last time I saw her – a tiny, wizened creature with her face turned towards the wall. I sat down next to the bed but she didn't turn to face me. I didn't tell her anything either because I discovered that I didn't need to. I wondered why it had ever been important for me to tell this woman about my life.

A memory flicked through my brain. A crowd of people yelling. Me in a stroller, sitting in a wet nappy with my bare feet sticking out of a pair of threadbare pants two sizes too small. Maybe it was Canberra. I remembered dry hills and a bitter wind. And an old woman with a powdered face and a blue perm who looked Mum up and down in the way old ladies did in those days. As if they had the right.

'You ought to be ashamed of yourself,' she'd said. 'Take that child home and put her into some warm clothes.'

And I'd screwed my head around and stared up at my mother as if to add my own small weight to the old woman's words. Although I knew well enough, even then, that my mother had neither home nor warm clothes to offer me, even if she'd wanted to.

I stared down at the twisted creature in the bed. If I ever have children, I thought, I won't treat them the way she treated us, Zara and me. Dragging us around from camp to camp, from squat to squat, and never enough to eat or clothes to wear. It was no way to bring up kids and expect them to love you in the end.

And I'd tried to please her, God knows I'd tried. Sometimes I thought the whole Brightsward thing was just part of that futile attempt to get her to notice me. Approve of me. Whatever.

Look at me, Mum. I'm just like you.

But now I realised that what I'd wanted from my mother all my life was something she'd never been capable of giving. A tear fell onto the white sheet. I watched the small damp circle fade into nothingness as I sniffed the rest away. Then I got up stiffly from the chair and looked down on my mother for what I knew was the last time.

'I guess you got what you deserved,' I said, harshly.

Not the stroke, I didn't mean that. Nobody deserved that fate, not even this old woman. More that she would spend the rest of her life alone, and unloved.

When I got back to Zara's place she was on the computer checking her emails. As I passed behind her chair, she moved the cursor to close down the page but it was too late. A name sprang out from the list in her Inbox. Annie Cormack. I felt my face flare red as I dumped the DVD I'd hired on the coffee table and went into the kitchen to make tea. In my mind I heard my grandmother's voice, *Let her have it, Zoe, she's the youngest*, as Zara helped herself to my meagre possessions. Clothes, make-up, boy friends, she'd had the lot and, in the end, I'd stopped caring. But this was going too far. I went back into the lounge room and sat down heavily in what had been Derek's recliner chair. Caution told me to leave it alone, but I wasn't listening.

'Seen the light at last, Zara?'

'What do you mean?' My sister had the grace to look uncomfortable.

'I thought you might have joined Brightsward.'

'No, of course not. Why would I do a thing like that?'

'So why are you getting emails from Annie Cormack?'

'Annie?' Zara glanced at the computer screen, now showing a picture of the two girls playing in the back yard. 'She came here looking for you, just after you'd left for Brisbane. It was the day Derek had to go to the police station because he'd dinged the car. She ended up staying a couple of nights. Looked after the kids while I was running around town trying to sort things out. It wasn't easy, you know, Zoe.'

'No, I don't suppose it was.'

Another glance at the screen. 'I get an email from her now and then, just to make sure I'm okay. She's *nice*, Zoe. For a …'

'For a *what*, Zara? Yeah, she's nice. Being gay doesn't have anything to do with it.'

Zara shrugged. 'Well, I've never met one before. Not that I knew about anyway. Now go and make that tea, if you're going to. Or open a bottle of wine. There's a cold one in the fridge.'

Martin rang after the girls had gone to bed and we were settling down to watch the DVD. Zara hit the pause button on the remote, then pretended not to listen while I took the call.

'Hey, Zoe, how's it going?'

'I'm looking forward to coming home.' I glanced at Zara but she was staring studiously at the paused image on the TV screen.

'That's what I was ringing for, to check the time of your flight.'

'Four thirty I get in.'

'Good oh. Oh, yes, and I've got some news for you.'

'What kind of news?'

'Something we can add to what we know about that MMC Institute of yours. Seems it owns the property next door to our farm. You remember? You and Dad flew over in the helicopter.'

'You're kidding.' I sat up straight, the phone clamped to my ear. 'How did you find that out?'

'I saw Dad yesterday. He'd come to town to do a search on the property. He's got a few fences down and he needed to talk to the owner about repairs.'

'He could have done that on the Internet.'

'Well, yeah, he probably could. But he doesn't mind an excuse to visit the big smoke every now and again. Anyway, there it was in black and white. The MMC Research Institute, registered in New York. We had lunch together and he was going off about foreign ownership of Australian soil.'

'So what does a research institute in New York want with a block of land in western Queensland?'

'I dunno, Zoe. Except they're building greenhouses on it.'

'Greenhouses?'

'That's what Dad said. Acres of them apparently. They went through town on big trucks a couple of weeks ago. Tons of steel and glass.'

'Yes, but greenhouses, Martin! That's truly bizarre. But I don't think it's going to help us with our hypothesis. In fact I'm not sure we've even got one any more.'

'Why? What's happened?'

I glanced again at Zara, still glued to the flickering image on the TV screen. 'I'll tell you about it when I get home, okay?'

'Okay, see you tomorrow then. Love you.'

And he hung up.

Zara flicked the button and the movie began again. 'Everything all right?'

'Yeah, fine. Martin was just checking my flight times.'

'What was all that about greenhouses? I thought Martin's dad ran a sheep property.'

'No, the greenhouses are on the property next door.'

'So why did your boy friend ring you up and tell you about greenhouses? You must have better things to talk about.'

'Because, strangely enough, those greenhouses might have a connection with my helicopter accident.'

'What kind of connection?' Zara reached for the remote and turned down the sound on the TV.

'You remember Colin Wilson? He was the one who died in the crash.'

'What about him?'

'Colin was in the Antarctic doing research into climate change. He was being funded by an institute in the US. And now Martin has discovered that this institute has bought a property in Quilpie and is putting greenhouses on it. Weird, eh?'

Zara dragged her eyes from the TV screen and turned to face me. 'You're not still obsessing about that accident, are you? Why can't you just leave it alone?'

'Colin died, Zara. Don't you think I should try and find out why?'

'It was an *accident*, Zoe. How many times do I have to tell you?'

I shook my head. 'No, it wasn't. He was murdered.'

'So you and this boy friend of yours are playing detective, is that it?' Zara narrowed her eyes. 'What are you up to, Zoe?'

'I'm not up to anything.'

'Well, it looks to me like you are. Poking your nose into things that don't concern you. You could get yourself into big trouble the way you're carrying on.'

'I'd like to clear my name,' I said steadily. 'So I can go back to my career.'

'Flying helicopters? That's not a career.' Zara shook her head impatiently. 'Take a look at yourself, Zoe. Don't you think it's time you started taking life seriously?'

'Live like you, you mean? Never happy unless you're buying stuff. Sometimes I wonder how you can be my sister.'

'Because I behave like a responsible adult instead of some overgrown teenager? Grow up, Zoe.' Zara flicked up the sound on the TV. 'Now are we going to watch this movie or aren't we?'

I sat and watched the bright images flickering on the screen while I waited for my rage to dissipate. I wondered how long it would be before I finally stopped firing up at my sister's attempts to run my life. After all, it was the same argument we had every time and it always came down to the same thing. She didn't understand me and I didn't understand her. And we didn't mention it again, not then and not in the morning either when she dropped me at the bus station for the ride to the airport. Ending the visit with a fight was so normal it didn't need any comment.

I arrived home to the smell of burning chops. Martin was sitting at the kitchen table engrossed with Alexander. I pulled the pan off the stove and dumped the chops in the bin where they sizzled among last week's vegetable peelings, then opened the fridge door and peered inside looking for something else to cook.

'Did your dad bring you a whole sheep?'

Martin looked up and grinned. 'Pretty much.'

'Well, I don't feel like lamb tonight. Let's get pizza. My shout.' I hooked a bottle of wine out of the box on top of the fridge and balanced it on the table among Martin's mess of papers. 'I'm going to buy myself a computer.'

Martin pushed his books to one side. 'Why?'

'My sister's got one.'

'Sibling rivalry, eh?'

'No, not sibling rivalry, Martin. It's just that I thought why not? We can hook it up to the Internet and you can do your work at home. That'd be okay, wouldn't it?'

'Not if you keep talking to me.'

'Come on, Martin. I've been away for three days. What's Alexander got that I haven't got?'

'You'd be surprised.' Martin stood up and enfolded me in his arms. 'But you've got something I might be interested in later.'

'You wish.' I smiled, then pushed him away. 'What sort of pizza do you want?'

After dinner we sat at the kitchen table drinking tea while I told Martin about Derek and his Internet sluts.

'… so if Dr Maddern's death really was a hit and run, I don't reckon we've got a hypothesis at all.'

Martin frowned. 'Why do you say that?'

'Look, Martin, I've been thinking. So far all this theory stuff has been about what we think, not what we know, right? And fair enough to begin with. You explained that we had to start with an idea. But now, if you look at the facts, what have we actually got?'

'Yes but we can't chuck the whole thing away just because one part of it doesn't work.' Martin grinned. 'What you're doing is testing the hypothesis. We'll make an academic of you yet.'

'So how do we … test the hypothesis?'

'We look at what we *do* know. The facts, if you want to call them that.'

'Okay. We know my helicopter was shot down because of that x-ray of my leg. We know Colin died.' I paused. 'I can't think of anything else.'

'There's plenty more.' Martin was counting on his fingers. 'We know Colin's research was funded by this MMC Research Institute in New York. We know the institute is connected with Brightsward. We know the institute has bought a property in Queensland and is putting greenhouses on it, though I have absolutely no idea why …'

'Martin, I've just thought of something else.' I glanced at the kitchen drawer. 'We've got Colin's data.'

'And?'

'Maybe we should take a look at it.'

'What for?'

'It'll tell us what he discovered.'

There was a long silence while Martin contemplated my words. Then, 'That's brilliant! An excellent idea.' He leaned forward and kissed me long and hard.

I grinned, pleased with his praise. 'Do you think you'd

be able to get Jamie away from his mozzies for a couple of hours tomorrow morning?'

'What do you want Jamie for?'

'We need him to interpret the data. Unless you'd like to have a go? And I'm going to ring Mr Wilson, too.' Then, before Martin could ask the question, 'His son was murdered because of what's on that memory stick. Don't you think he's got a right to know why he died?'

ELEVEN

Mr Wilson arrived first, carrying his brand-new laptop computer. By the time we'd cleared a space on the table and set it up, Jamie turned up with his hair spiked up with gel although, judging by his crumpled track pants and stained hoodie, that was all he'd done to greet the day. He looked a little dazed by the bright morning sun and stepped into our gloomy house like a hermit returning to his cave. I put the kettle on while the men gathered around the computer. At a word from Jamie, Martin retrieved the memory stick from its hiding place in the cutlery drawer and pushed it into the USB port.

There was silence while Jamie scrolled through the files. I brought the mugs to the table and found a space between the heads where I could see the computer screen. Not that it did me much good. Jamie, however, was nodding his head and making noises that seemed to indicate understanding as he flicked between the screens.

Finally he looked up. 'Does anyone have any idea what Colin was trying to do in Antarctica?'

'He was looking for a bacterial marker to monitor sea temperature changes,' I said, causing all the heads to swivel in my direction.

Jamie nodded. 'Okay, so a micro-organism that would behave differently when the temperature of the water increased beyond its range?'

'Die, dwindle or decamp. That's what Professor McRae said it would do.'

Jamie grinned. 'That was one of his favourite sayings. Must have heard it a hundred times.' He grabbed his mug and took a swig of the hot tea. 'Not that any of Colin's bugs were behaving that way. Or, at least, not consistently.'

'You're saying the bacteria weren't doing what he thought they would do?'

'Not all of them. Some behaved themselves quite nicely and died off just when he said they would. But he's got a bunch of bacteria living happily and not caring that they're swimming in a warm bath. According to his theory, they should have been as dead as mutton.'

'So what do you do in a situation like that?'

Jamie grinned again. He was enjoying himself. 'Plenty you can do. Change bugs, change what you do to them, change hypothesis, or give up and go home. Hey, mate?'

He swivelled his head around and stared up at Martin.

Martin nodded. 'You stick with your theory, if you can. But you need the evidence to back it up.'

'So what did Colin do?' I asked.

'I'm not sure.' Jamie turned back to the computer. 'For some reason, he ditched the temperature tests and started experimenting with salinity.'

'I think I can help you there,' said Mr Wilson. He reached into his computer bag and came up with a battered exercise book which he laid carefully on the table. 'This was in a box of Colin's things that was sent from Casey Station not long after he died. I didn't fancy looking through them when they first arrived, so I shoved the box into his room and tried to forget about it. But when Miss Carter – Zoe – rang me last night I thought there might be something in there that would be useful.'

Jamie's eyes lit up. 'Colin's research diary. Here, give me that.'

Mr Wilson pointed his big, soft finger. 'You'll find a reference to salinity about half way through.'

Jamie bent his head and began flicking through the pages. 'Is this the bit you mean? *I've been talking to Brad, the oceanographer from Monash, about my experiments and it looks like I've missed something important. He said I should check where my aberrant samples came from. I have been* taking samples from the surface and deeper down to allow for temperature variations and Brad reminded me of something I should have remembered from Grade 12 science – that fresh water is less dense than salty water. He told me to test the salinity of the water in my samples and he's right. The bacteria that are unaffected by changes in temperature come from a brackish layer at the surface of the water.' Jamie reached up his hands and pulled at his blond spikes. 'So that blasts a big, fat hole in Colin's research.'

'Why?' I asked

'Because it adds another variable. How is he going to prove an organism is affected by rising temperatures when it's being affected by something else as well?'

'Colin didn't get himself murdered for being wrong,' growled Mr Wilson. 'Give it here.' He reached out his big soft hand and took the book. Flicked the pages. 'Here. We're into early December now. *I've finally had an answer from Professor McRae. He sent me a paper of some work that was carried out in a tidal estuary in Portugal and it confirms my findings. Prof thinks we could use my bugs as a marker for decreasing salinity in the Southern Ocean. He wants me to write it up as soon as I get back to Australia.'*

'But I thought Colin was supposed to be finding a measure for global warming,' I said, puzzled. 'How's that going to work if his bacteria are testing for salinity?' And then I realised. 'Oh yes, of course. Melting ice caps. That's what I was doing in the Antarctic, taking pictures of them falling apart.'

'But it still doesn't explain why Colin got himself killed,' said Martin. 'None of this stuff is exactly new.'

'Can I look?'

I turned to Mr Wilson and he handed me Colin's diary. Holding the book in my hands, I could almost smell the fusty warmth of the Antarctic dongas and the sharp tang of the ice. With trembling hands, I began to turn the pages. Somewhere in this tattered exercise book was the answer I had been seeking ever since I found out my helicopter had been shot out of the sky. Why Colin died.

Finally I looked up. 'Listen to this. *Brad is really excited about my discovery because he is modelling currents in the Atlantic and water density plays an important role in how they function. He has been re-running his computer models based on a rapid desalination of water in the Southern Ocean caused by melt water, and he has come up with an unexpected result. Apparently the density of the water in the Southern Ocean is crucial to the pumping mechanism of what he calls the Atlantic conveyer belt. The Gulf Stream to everybody else. Whatever it's called, Brad says it delivers warm water to Europe that heats the air by about 5°C.*

Here's the point. Northern Europe is at the same latitude as Canada and it is only the warm water carried from the tropics by the Gulf Stream that keeps its temperature relatively mild. If the pump slows, or fails, because of a change in sea water salinity in the Southern Ocean, Europe will get colder. Rapidly colder. And we aren't talking hundreds of years here. More like ten. So it's scary stuff.

I've asked Brad to collaborate with me on the paper Professor McRae wants me to write. I don't suppose Prof will be too happy about having another author on the paper but that's his hard luck. I'm going to email my last lot of data to MMC tonight and then I can relax. It's Midsummer Eve tomorrow and we're having a party.'

I clutched the diary to my chest. Within three – no, four – days of that entry Colin was dead and I was in a US hospital with a bullet in my leg. There was a long silence in the room.

Then, 'Far out,' said Jamie.

'But it's the other fellow, this Brad person, who was doing research on the ocean currents,' said Mr Wilson. 'So why did they kill my boy?'

'It's the same old story,' said Martin, looking towards Jamie for confirmation. 'It's not about what's going to happen but when. That's the important thing.'

Jamie nodded. 'Colin came up with a test for salinity which has the potential to pin-point the exact moment when the ocean pumps will begin to fail.'

Mr Wilson sat down suddenly. 'And someone needed that test kept secret because they want to profit from this big freeze in Europe? Is that what you're saying?'

'Pretty much.'

'So now we've got a motive for Colin's murder.'

'And for Professor McRae's,' said Martin, 'because he was going to publish Colin's findings.'

'Hang on,' said Jamie. 'What's this about murder? I thought Prof died of a heart attack.'

'It looked like a heart attack,' I said. 'But it's too much of a coincidence that he dropped dead all by himself at that precise moment.'

'Yes, I'd agree with that,' said Mr Wilson. 'I thought the same thing the other day when you told me he was dead.'

'So what killed him?' asked Jamie. 'If he didn't drop dead by himself?'

'Could have been poison,' I said.

'An untraceable poison,' said Mr Wilson, 'if he ended up with 'heart attack' as the cause of death.'

And Martin said, 'In that case he was probably killed by a woman.'

Jamie raised an eye brow. 'A woman? What makes you think that?'

'Poison is a woman's weapon. Men tend to bash, or stab, or shoot. The ladies prefer a less violent means of dispatching their victims.' Martin nodded towards his picture of Alexander blu-tacked to the kitchen wall. 'His mother Olympias got rid of one or two that way.'

Jamie laughed. 'Maybe there's something in this ancient history crap, after all.'

But I wasn't listening. A woman, I thought. Suddenly all the pieces clicked into place, one by one, and I knew who it was. Who it must be. I remembered telling Martin I felt like I was being stalked. And I had been. Everywhere I went, she went. Even to my sister's house in Bowen.

I said, 'Martin, remember that girl who came to visit me the day you wrecked the screen door? What did she look like?'

Apprehension clouded Martin's face. 'Zoe, that was weeks ago!'

'Okay, let me make it easier for you. My height? Short red hair? American accent?'

'Yes, that's her.'

I turned to Mr Wilson. 'Ring any bells with you?'

He nodded slowly. 'That sounds like the girl from the institute who brought us those flowers.'

'Then it was Annie Cormack,' I said. 'And listen to this. She was in Bowen when Dr Maddern was killed. My sister told me.' Then, before Martin opened his mouth to speak,' Well, maybe the cops got it wrong about Derek. It wouldn't be the first time.' A quick glance at Mr Wilson. 'And Annie knew about my x-ray because I told her myself. I met her not long after I'd had my surgery.'

I ground to a halt, too appalled to continue. It was like I'd signed Dr Maddern's death warrant. But Mr Wilson was watching me carefully.

'Keep going.'

'Then she came down here. She was in Brisbane when your computer was stolen. First she brought you those stinky flowers, then she broke into your house and took your computer, then she came to visit me.'

'That means she was in Brisbane when Professor McRae died as well,' said Martin. 'Was she following you, d'you think?'

I shook my head miserably. 'I think it's more likely we both went to the same places for the same reason. Looking for Colin's data.'

Mr Wilson turned to Jamie. 'Where was Professor McRae found?'

'In his office.'

'Door open or shut?'

'Shut. He was lying behind it. They had to force it open.'

'Are you going back to the lab today?'

Jamie nodded. 'I'm teaching at eleven.'

Can you get a swab from the inside handle of Professor McRae's door? Be very careful. We don't know how potent the stuff is.' Then Mr Wilson turned to me. 'And you said this Annie Cormack came to visit you?'

I nodded.

'So when was that in relation to Professor McRae's death?'

'It could have been the same day. Professor McRae was found the following morning.'

'She was taking a risk, then. Two so close together. But nobody would make the connection between you and Professor McRae, would they? Two random deaths, that's how they'd appear. And her on a plane to New York.'

Martin laid his warm hands on my shoulders. 'Are you saying Annie Cormack came to this house to kill Zoe?'

Mr Wilson nodded. 'That's exactly what I'm saying.'

'Okay, fair enough. But why didn't she?'

I turned my head. 'I wasn't home, remember?'

'No, but if she was painting stuff on door handles ...'

And suddenly there was the memory, as clear as crystal. The screen door broken off its hinges. Martin crashing about in the kitchen looking for keys. Mad because Annie had made him miss his bus.

My eyes widened in horror. 'Martin, the screen door!'

We all crowded out of the house and stared at the old screen door still leaning drunkenly against the dark green bush where it had fallen after Martin wrenched it off its hinges.

'Well, well, what do we have here?' Mr Wilson bent forward stiffly and peered through the mesh at the dry, dead leaves still clustered around the door handle.

We explained, the three of us, because Jamie had been there, too, when he and Martin had come home from uni with the news of Professor McRae's death.

'You were pretty mad,' I said to Martin. 'It's not like you to get angry like that.'

Martin grinned sheepishly. 'I had a meeting with my supervisor, that's why, and I hadn't got anything new to show her. I needed a good session in the library to catch up.'

'He always was the teacher's pet,' grinned Jamie.

Mr Wilson turned his head. 'Zoe, have you got a plastic bag?'

'I'll go.' Martin went into the house.

Mr Wilson reached carefully around the door, pinched off a small bunch of the dead leaves between thumb and finger and dropped them carefully into the plastic bag that Martin held open for him. He wiped his hand on the seat of his pants.

'Come on, then,' he said to Jamie. 'Let's go and get that sample from the professor's door. I'm going to call in a few favours from the forensic boys, see what they come up with. Maybe we'll have some answers by tomorrow morning.'

The next morning we gathered on campus in the refectory where I'd first met Martin. We found a table by the window and I watched the chilly wind blowing paper around outside while Martin fetched the hot brown liquid they served as coffee. The room was full of students and the roar of their voices was like a shield protecting us from prying ears. When the polystyrene cups were on the table Mr Wilson turned his head from side to side, scanning the room, then pulled his chair in closer.

'It was poison all right,' he said. 'A synthetic derivative of Ricin that kills on contact with the skin and degrades very quickly. We were lucky there was enough left to get a positive swab.'

'So what's the idea?' I asked. 'You paint it on a door knob and the first person to touch it dies instantly but nobody else does?'

'That's right.' Mr Wilson nodded. 'And it was placed very carefully. On the handle inside Professor McRae's office so only he would touch it when he went into his office and closed the door. And on the handle to the screen door, so you'd touch it when you came home.'

'You reckon Annie knew I was out?' I said.

Another nod. 'She probably watched you go.'

'And then I came out of the back room and found her on the door step,' said Martin. 'I must have given her the fright of her life.'

'She would have given you more than a fright, if you'd touched that handle,' said Mr Wilson.

'Oh, my God.' My eyes were wide with distress. 'Martin, you could have died.' I leaned forward and buried my face in my outstretched hands. 'I don't believe this.'

Martin laid his arm heavily across my shoulders.

'Come on, Zoe. Don't cry.'

'I'm not crying.' I shrugged off his hand and lifted my head. 'But it's true. You could have died. And it would have been my fault.'

'Let's get one thing straight, Zoe. None of this is your fault.' Mr Wilson reached forward and emptied two packets of sugar into his coffee. Stirred carefully. 'And now we've got something else to deal with. The boys from the anti-terrorism squad are very interested in our poison. It's never been found on Australian soil before and they want to know where I got it.' He looked round the table. 'I haven't told them anything yet. But I won't be able to keep them off my back for long. They're very nervous people right now.'

'But we can't tell them,' I said. 'Not yet.'

'But, Zoe, if the police can gather enough evidence to convict this Annie person of murder, we can get the inquest reopened. You'll be able to go back to flying. Isn't that what you want?'

I placed my coffee cup very carefully onto the table and watched as some of the brown liquid slopped out onto the sticky surface.

'It *was* what I wanted, Mr Wilson. But, you know what? It just got personal.' I reached out and grabbed Martin's hand. 'Annie came to Queensland to get rid of Colin's data. And to kill me. She almost killed Martin. So now I'm going to nail her. Personally.'

'But why did Annie want to kill you?' asked Jamie. 'You only found out about Colin's discovery yesterday. The same as the rest of us.'

I turned my head. 'Because I was with Colin when he died. I don't think I was supposed to survive the crash. Someone stuffed up, otherwise I'd never have made it out of Antarctica alive.'

'You took a risk going to New York.'

'I thought it was the safest place in the world.' I glanced at Martin. 'It never occurred to me that someone connected with Brightsward was responsible for Colin's death. I still find it hard to believe.'

'And Annie took a risk inviting you,' said Mr Wilson thoughtfully. 'Any idea why she did it?'

'To have a look at me. That's what I reckon. To see if I was still a threat. Which I obviously wasn't because here I am in Brisbane talking to you guys.'

'You were lucky, then.' Jamie gulped down the rest of his coffee. 'Look, guys, I've got to go. I've got a tutorial with a bunch of First Years. If any of them bother to show up.'

'And I've got a phone call to make. I'm still not sure what I'm going to say.' Mr Wilson put his big hands flat on the table and heaved himself to his feet. 'Zoe, do you want a lift home? I've got my car somewhere on a parking meter. I hope I can manage to find it again.'

We were silent on the short journey but, when we were parked outside the house, Mr Wilson turned to me and said, 'Now then, young lady, what am I going to tell the police?'

I turned my head sharply. 'How much will satisfy them?'

Mr Wilson scrutinised my face. 'I'd like to give them everything but you're not going to let me do that, are you?'

I shook my head.

'So what are you planning to do?'

'I'm going back to New York.'

Mr Wilson sighed. 'I thought as much. Look, Zoe, you survived the last time. Why go back and give Annie another chance to have a go at you?'

'I reckon I'm safe enough' I said with more confidence than I was feeling. 'Look, Mr Wilson, as far as Annie's concerned I'm just sad old Zoe Carter, the Brightsward groupie who won't take no for an answer. But the minute you talk to the police, I'll have a big red target on my forehead that nobody can miss.'

Mr Wilson thought for a while, then he said, 'You're right. We can't take the risk.' He stared out of the windscreen at the white scuff marks on the river, tossed up by the cold wind. 'How about this? I'll give them Professor McRae's murder. Hint at a disgruntled student from foreign lands. That should hold them for a while.'

I grinned. 'Thanks, Mr Wilson.' I opened the car door. 'I'll see you later, okay?'

Mr Wilson leaned towards me – a sudden impulse, followed by a second's hesitation. Then he planted a brief kiss on my cheek. I could smell the stale coffee on his breath.

'You're a brave girl,' he said. 'Just make sure you keep in touch with that young man of yours.'

'First I've got to tell him I'm going.'

TWELVE

I bought a computer and hooked it up to the Internet. Then I sent an email to Madeleine. Once he had given up trying to stop me going to New York, it was Martin who came up with a plausible reason for my trip. Like all the best lies, it was very simple.

From: zoe@gmail.com
To: m.vaneps@brightsward.com
Cc:
Subject: Hope to see you soon!

Hi Madeleine
I found a really cheap flight on the Internet so I am coming back to New York! This time as a tourist so I can see all the things I missed out on last time. I hope we can catch up during my stay.
See you soon,
Zoe.

I didn't have to wait long for a reply. And it came from Annie.

From: a.cormack@brightsward.com
To: zoe@gmail.com
Cc:
Subject: RE: Hope to see you soon!

Hi Zoe
Madeleine mentioned to her grandfather that you are planning a visit to New York and he asked me to invite you to come and visit with us during your stay. Eric is still not well so I hope you don't mind receiving this invitation

from me. If you let me know when you are due to touch
down at JFK, I will send Johannes with the car.
Looking forward to seeing you soon,
Annie.

Bingo, I thought, when Annie's email dropped into my
Inbox. It was a strange thing to be pleased about: an invitation
from a girl who, only a few weeks ago, was trying to kill me
stone dead. But I booked my flight – the first one I could get
on to – and then I had three days to spend with Martin.

He pushed his books aside and we dragged some old
chairs into the unkempt garden and sat holding hands in
the warm sunshine. We took the City Cat to South Bank and
walked along by the river. We went to New Farm park and
had a picnic in the patchy shade of the old trees. We told
each other about our childhoods and talked about the books
we'd read and the movies we liked. But we didn't talk about
the future and we didn't mention New York. And it was
only the slow-burning anger deep within my soul stoked by
the image of Martin's body slumped on the door step, dead
from Annie Cormack's poison, that gave me the strength to
carry on with a plan that my heart was screaming at me not
to do.

On the third day we took a cab to the airport. After my
bags had been checked in, we sat at a small table staring at
each other miserably while two expensive cappuccinos went
cold between us. When it was time to move, Martin reached
into his pocket and held out a dog-eared paperback book.

'I want you to take this.'

I knew what it was – a history of Alexander written by
some ancient bloke called Arrian. Living with Martin meant
that I lived with Arrian, too. How often had I watched
Martin working at the old table by the kitchen window,
while I cooked dinner, or washed up, or made tea - all the
things I said I'd never, ever do. Watched his long, deft fingers
flicking through the pages looking for the words he surely
knew by heart. Watched the way he turned swiftly to scrawl
something on his scruffy note pad.

I took the book and held it to my nose. It smelled of old

paper and mozzie coils and dinners long gone. 'This is your Arrian,' I said. 'Why are you giving it to me?'

'I want you to have it so you won't forget me. It's my most precious possession. *Was* my most precious possession.' He reached for my hands and gripped them hard. 'I love you, Zoe. You know that, don't you?'

But I didn't reply. I'd never said those words to anyone in my life and I couldn't say them now. Of course I loved him. More than anything. But that didn't make the words any easier to say.

We stood at the top of the escalator leading down to the departure lounge. Now it was time to leave, I didn't want to let him go.

'I'll miss you.

'I'll miss you, too.'

'Come back soon.'

'I will.'

But, as I rode down the escalator, I wondered how long it would be before I saw him again.

It was hot in New York. The trees outside Eric's house were drooping under a layer of grime. Inside, I was greeted by an oppressive silence. There was no welcoming smile from Annie, which was just as well because I still didn't know how I was going to handle meeting her again. Celeste escorted me upstairs to the guest bedroom and brought me a tray of tea with a pretty china cup. I unpacked and lay on my bed until the connecting door opened and Madeleine came tip-toeing into the room.

'You're not asleep are you?'

I struggled to sit up. 'Not any more. How are you, Madeleine?'

'Good. Real good.' Her face split into a smile of real pleasure. 'It's great to see you again, Zoe. You wanna come into my room? I've got something for you.'

No guesses what it's going to be, I thought, as I swung my legs off the bed and followed Madeleine through the door. And sure enough there was Madeleine's little tin of rollie paper lying on the window sill next to a plastic bag of weed.

'Good old Dimitri, eh?' I said as I accepted the joint from her long fingers. I inhaled and felt the smoke hit my stomach sickeningly and it wasn't just the jet lag either. I wasn't used to the stuff any more, that was the truth of it. When Madeleine held it out to me again I shook my head.

She shot me a look. 'You okay?'

'Yeah, I'm fine. I just don't feel like smoking, that's all.'

'That's crap.' Her eyes displayed their usual innocence but, behind them, she was watching me closely. 'It's Annie, isn't it? She's warned you off.'

'I haven't even seen her, Madeleine.'

'Not now. Last time. What did she say to you?'

'She said you smoked too much pot. And she's right.

A long stream of blue smoke. 'I'll do what I like.' Madeleine stubbed out the joint on the window sill and stowed the butt in her little tin. 'What I should do is leave a syringe for her to find. That's what she's waiting for. Hoping for, probably.'

'Why would she be hoping for something like that?'

'Annie thinks I'm gonna end up like my mom, shooting my grandfather's money into my arm. I guess she's waiting for it to happen so she can prove to Opa how useless I am.'

'I don't see what it's got to do with Annie what you do.'

Another glance from those dark, fathomless eyes. 'Haven't you worked it out yet, Zoe? Everything is to do with Annie around here.' She turned away from the window. 'Do you want to go and see Opa?'

'Does he know I'm here?'

'Probably not. But we can go and see him anyway.'

'Where is he?'

'In his bedroom. Where he always is these days.' She slid off the bed and went to the bathroom to gargle and sluice her face with cold water. 'Come on.'

We crossed the corridor and Madeleine knocked softly on Eric's door, then opened it just wide enough for us to slide in. The blinds were pulled down over the windows and the room was stiflingly hot. Eric was huddled in an armchair next to the unmade bed. He had a thick woollen blanket wrapped around his shoulders and an electric heater on the floor in front of him, pumping hot air onto his slipper-clad feet.

114

I was shocked by his appearance. He had lost weight and lost it quickly. His big, jowly face was shrunken, his eyes sunk deep in greyish skin. His hair was thin and coarse against his freckled scalp. He showed little interest in my visit nor in Madeleine's plans for my entertainment. The only time he showed any animation was at the end of the interview when he leaned forward in his chair and insisted we make sure the door was closed properly when we left.

'It's the drafts, you see,' he said querulously. 'I can't stand the drafts round my feet.'

By then I was sweating in the over-heated room and I was only too pleased to shake his hot, dry hand and escape into the relative cool of the corridor.

Despite my jet lag, sleep eluded me that night as I lay sweating on top of the sheets. Even with the windows wide open there was no air stirring the curtains. Beyond my closed door, I was aware of the close, stuffy, sick-room atmosphere of the house. Quiet voices. Doors closing softly. The quick tap of feet in the corridor. Finally I swung my legs out of bed and padded over the thick carpet to the window. I leaned my elbows on the sill and stared blankly at the thin strip of lurid sky that lay above the opposite building. So remind me, I thought, what am I doing here? It had been easy enough planning Annie's destruction in a Queensland university refectory, fifteen hours away on the other side of the world. Now I was here, I didn't know where to begin. For a start, Annie was away, or so Celeste had told me. Gone to a conference in Washington, DC. Back on Friday night.

The day before I flew out, Mr Wilson and I had met briefly in the food court of the shopping centre near the university, eating pizza out of a cardboard box while his wife was at the hairdressers.

'Your best bet is to find out what you can about the institute,' he'd said. 'Don't waste your time with Brightsward headquarters. It might be MMC's registered address but there won't be anything there except a plaque on the wall.' He reached into the box for another slice of pizza. 'It's my guess there's a laboratory somewhere. That poison Annie used on Professor McRae was synthetic. You don't buy stuff like that off a supermarket shelf.'

'You mean she made it herself?'

'She did or somebody else did.' He dropped the half-eaten slice of pizza back into the box and leaned forward. 'When I was a cop we always knew when law-abiding citizens were cooking up drugs in their back kitchens, no matter what their fancy lawyers tried to tell us. You could smell it on their skin. But it wasn't a smell you'd notice unless you were looking for it.' He wiped his mouth with a paper napkin. 'So watch her, that's what I'm saying. Find out where she goes, what she does, who she sees. Straws in the wind, that's what you're looking for. *Any* clue, no matter how small. But be careful, Zoe. It makes no difference if you catch Annie or the cops do. What matters is that you come home safe.'

But, with Annie out of the house for the next few days, what was I going to do in the mean time? It was no good trying to talk to Eric, he was far too sick even to tolerate a five minute visit. Which left Little Miss Pot-head in the room next door who appeared to have been side-lined from anything that happened in the house or at Brightsward. Annie didn't like Madeleine, that was obvious. Apart from her disapproval of Madeleine's drug habit, she thought she was a spoiled brat who got things too easy. And the feeling was mutual. But what was the reason for Madeleine's hostility towards Annie? Madeleine was a nice kid and she was lonely. She didn't seem to have a problem getting along with me. So what was going on between the two of them? What had Annie done to make Madeleine dislike her so much? I stood upright and let the curtains fall into place over the window. Maybe over the next few days I'd have a chance to find out.

So where's the first place a tourist goes in New York city? For me it was the Statue of Liberty which I thought said New York the way the Harbour Bridge says Sydney. Johannes dropped us at the ferry stop straight after breakfast but, even that early in the morning, there were a couple of hundred people in the queue that snaked along the water front from the ticket office. Wearing a flimsy floral skirt and a fresh white blouse, her pale complexion protected by a wide straw hat, Madeleine was like an exotic butterfly as we waited in line with the foreign backpackers and American tourists. In front of us a mid-west family, as wide as they were tall, were sweating pure lard into the steamy air. And, of course, we had to endure their company in the close atmosphere of the ferry's cabin during the ride to Liberty Island.

It was my choice to sit inside. Blame my north Queensland upbringing that I didn't want to sit in the sun. Just as it was my choice to visit the statue on our first day, not realising we had to have a special pass to get into the pedestal where the museum was, something we needed to reserve two days in advance. I knew we wouldn't be able to get into the statue itself. It had been closed to visitors since 2001, part of the post 9/11 paranoia that was still alive and well in New York city. Airport-style body searches before we even set foot on the island were evidence of that.

Still there was plenty to see and it was afternoon by the time we caught the ferry back to Manhattan and this time, anxious for some fresh air, we pushed our way to the bow and found a space at the railings. And there was fresh air galore as the boat ploughed its way through a rough chop kicked up by the afternoon breeze blowing off the sea. Every now and then a wave broke over the bow sending a cascade of chilly spray over the people standing against the rail.

As I braced my legs against the dip and sway of the deck, I was reminded of that amazing, hair-raising trip from Buenos Aires to McMurdo Sound on board the *Astral Traveller*. Those great grey seas of the Southern Ocean, the brief sensation of being airborne as the ship hung on the crest of a huge wave, followed by the bone-jarring crunch as she hit the bottom of the next trough. I remembered my fear for the safety of my beautiful new helicopter that was lashed firmly to the deck amidships, more firmly than the crew who were left to rattle around like peas in a cup. I stole a glance at Madeleine as the next curtain of spray drifted across. She was balanced lightly on her feet, her eyes gleaming with pleasure, her wet hair whipped across her face by the wind.

She turned her head. 'Pretty cool, huh?'

'You like rough sea? Try the *Astral Traveller* a day out from Chile.' And was instantly rewarded by the look of eager interest on her face.

'What was she like? I wish I'd had a chance to see her.'

I grinned. 'A rust bucket with a rainbow on the side.'

'Did you like the rainbow? That was my idea. And the name. I thought of that, too.'

Another thump from the ferry as it hit a wave head on. I grabbed Madeleine's arm as the cold spray drenched us.

'Come on, let's move. I'm getting soaked standing here.'

We pushed our way to the back of the foredeck and wedged ourselves in a space between a life belt and the cabin wall. I leaned on the railing and watched the green swell roll along the side of the ferry.

'I didn't know you were involved in planning the Antarctic trip,' I said. 'I thought you were Brightsward's publicity girl.'

'Well, yeah, I was but I helped Opa, too.' She pulled a strand of wet hair away from her face. 'We had a lot of fun, Opa and me, before he started getting sick.'

'When was that? Do you remember?'

'It started last spring when the *Astral Traveller* was still in Antarctica. Opa had promised me a trip down to Buenos Aires to see her when she got back but, by then, he was too sick and he wouldn't let me go by myself.'

'It seems a pity when you'd put so much work into the expedition.'

'I didn't do that much in the end. Opa gave the Antarctic trip to Annie. And Annie made it very clear she didn't want me around.'

I watched Madeleine's hands grip the rail, her knuckles showing white through her pale skin. Now we're getting somewhere, I thought.

The ferry was turning a semi-circle to come in to the dock, now in deep shade from Manhattan's tall buildings. The stifling afternoon heat reasserted itself as the wind died away. Around us people were getting ready to disembark. I turned around and leaned my back on the railings, staring up at the glittering skyline. Beyond Battery Park, Johannes would be waiting with the car to take us home. I didn't have much time.

'Where did Annie come from, Madeleine?'

'Off the streets.' She dragged both hands through her hair and twisted it behind her head. 'She just kinda showed up. Started making herself useful around the office.'

'A volunteer, then?'

A shrug. 'Brightsward runs on volunteers. There wasn't anything unusual about that.'

'And then?' I bent down and picked up my backpack from between my feet.

'She started getting into Opa's ear. I remember he used to bring her home for dinner and she'd sit next to him at the table, talking herself up.'

'What about?'

'Global warming was Annie's thing. She was full of big ideas.' Madeleine leaned on the railing and stared at the rubbish swilling up and down in the sullen water. 'I guess that's why she muscled her way into the Antarctic expedition.'

'Took it over?'

'U-huh.'

'What about you? What happened to you when Annie took over the project?'

'She kicked me off. That's what happened. Told Opa I was making too many mistakes and she didn't have time to fix them up. She'd brought the sailing day forward, see, because the ice shelves were breaking up earlier than expected.' Madeleine turned from the rail and we began following the crowd of people who were moving towards the gangplank. 'But it wasn't true, Zoe. I know I'm only a kid but I was working for Opa long before *she* turned up. I knew what I was doing.'

'So why did she say it?'

She turned her head and I could see the hurt in her eyes. 'She wanted me out of the way. She had plans of her own, that's what I reckon, and she didn't want me to find out what they were.'

'What sort of plans?'

She shrugged unhappily. 'You tell me. You were there.'

THIRTEEN

That evening Madeleine and I wedged open the door between our bedrooms so we could keep talking while we showered and changed for dinner. It was my first formal dinner since I arrived and I was surprised when we went into the dining room to see Eric's accustomed place set at the head of the table.

'Is Eric coming down for dinner?'

Madeleine shook her head. 'He hasn't been out of his room in weeks.'

'So what's with the table setting?' I pulled out the heavy wooden chair and sat down.

'Annie gets Celeste to set Opa's place every night. Just to show he's still the boss, I guess.' Madeleine sat down opposite me. 'It's weird, I know, but that's the way she is. Always acting like he's in charge and she's just doing as she's told.'

'And that's not true?'

'Of course it's not true. Zoe. Annie has Brightsward like this.' Madeleine lifted her hand, palm up and squeezed it into a tight fist.

We were silent while Celeste came in with our food and then, when she'd left the room, Madeleine said, 'Why are you here, Zoe?'

I looked up, startled, into her clear, green-flecked eyes. 'What do you mean?'

'You didn't come to New York to see the sights. So why are you here?' Madeleine picked up her fork and dug it viciously into her pasta. 'When you visited with us last time I thought you were Annie's friend. But I don't think that's true any more.' She looked up again. 'Are you my friend?'

'I ... I hope so.'

'Then talk to me. Tell me what's on your mind.'

Madeleine's voice held that attractive mixture of command and childish innocence I remembered from my last visit. But, still, I was not sure I could trust her. I picked up my fork and twirled it in my pasta. There was silence for a long moment.

Then Madeleine said, 'Come on, Zoe. Maybe I can help you. Maybe you can help *me*.' And there was that infinite sadness deep within her eyes.

I took a deep breath. 'When I crashed my helicopter someone died. His name was Colin Wilson. I think Colin was murdered and I want to know why.'

'So why come here?

'Because Annie had something to do with it. That's why.'

Madeleine nodded, unsurprised. 'What do you want to know?'

I leaned forward. 'What's she up to, Madeleine? Here in New York?'

Madeleine forked up a mouthful of pasta. 'What do you want? The official version? Or the truth.'

'The official version will do for a start.'

'Annie's developing a new direction for Brightsward. It's something she sold to Opa about a year and a half ago. Stop publicising the world's environmental problems and start doing something to solve them.'

I raised an eye brow. 'It's not such a bad idea. How did Eric take it?'

'He wasn't keen to begin with. Sure, it's a good idea, but Annie wanted a lot of cash to make it work. And I'm talking serious money.'

'So what changed his mind?'

'When she said it would pay for itself. A two-in-one package is how she explained it to Opa. Save the world and make money at the same time. Plough the profit back into Brightsward.' A forkful of food. 'She's got a degree in biochemistry, see, and she wanted to set up a bunch of labs. That's why she needed so much cash.'

My heart thumped with sudden excitement. 'And did she? Set up the labs, I mean.'

'Sure. They're down in New Jersey.'

'What sort of work are they doing?'

'The official version is anti-malarial drugs, pest management, water quality, that sort of thing.' Madeleine had given up on her fork and was using a spoon to scoop up the creamy sauce. 'Oh, yes, and food production. That's the one Opa liked the best. A kinda twenty-first century Green Revolution, you know?'

'And the truth?'

'That's what I'm not sure about. But it's big. And she's in a hurry.'

'How do you know?'

'She's spending a lot of money. A *lot* of money.' Madeleine looked up. There was a malicious gleam, now, at the back of her clear, green-flecked eyes. 'Annie thinks I'm Little Miss Nobody in this house but she forgets I talk to Opa. And he's worried. She's bleeding Brightsward dry.'

Celeste came in and cleared our plates, then returned with a bowl of fruit salad and a jug of cream which she placed between us. When she was gone I leaned forward and began spooning the fruit into our bowls.

'These labs,' I said. 'Do they operate under Brightsward's name?'

Madeleine pulled her bowl towards her.

'No, they've been set up as a commercial enterprise so officially they're a separate entity. Brightsward's a not-for-profit organisation so they have to be, otherwise the taxation department would be down on us like a ton of bricks.'

I poured cream over my fruit. 'So what name do they operate under?'

Madeleine shook her head. 'I don't know.'

'Have you ever heard of the MMC Research Institute?

Madeleine reached for the cream jug. 'No, never. What does it do?'

'It hands out research grants to scientists. And it's attached to Brightsward.'

Madeleine looked up, her spoon halfway to her mouth.

'And you think it might be the name Annie's using for the labs?'

'The thought did cross my mind.'

'So how do you know about it?'

'Colin. The boy who was riding in my helicopter. His research was funded by the MMC.'

'In Antarctica?' Madeleine raised an eyebrow. 'That's got to be a coincidence, right?'

'What do you mean?'

Well, it's kinda weird, anyway. You know it was Annie's idea to send you to Antarctica?'

'*Annie's* idea?'

'Sure. I remember her and Opa having a big argument about it at the dinner table. Annie told Opa she was going to appoint you as the helicopter pilot on the expedition and Opa wanted to know why she'd suddenly decided to use some cowboy from the outback of Australia instead of one of our regular guys.'

'I was a Brightsward member. And a good pilot. Why shouldn't she appoint me?'

'Opa said you didn't have enough experience. Not for flying in Antarctic conditions.'

'But Annie had her way.'

'Yeah, like I said. She usually does.' Madeleine smiled. 'I just thought you were some girl she'd met on her travels. She brings them home from time to time. But you're not gay, are you? You've got Martin.'

I shook my head. 'No, I'm not gay.' I grinned. 'And I don't think I'd fancy Annie, even if I was.'

At bed time Celeste brought me my tray of tea and I sat by the open window drinking it in the hope it would cool me down, while Madeleine leaned on the sill blowing pot smoke into the humid air.

She turned her head. 'Doesn't it make you hot?'

'The tea? No, it cools you down.' I grinned. 'You should give it a try.'

It was an old north Queensland habit I'd picked up from my grandmother. I remembered her on hot summer nights sitting on the back steps with her skirt hitched up over her knees supping hot tea from a cracked mug while the lightening crackled in the dark sky over the cane fields.

'Anyway, I'm off to bed.' I put the empty cup on the tray. 'All that fresh air has worn me out. See you in the morning.'

But once again sleep eluded me. As soon as I closed my eyes my brain started churning. Going over everything Madeleine had said to me that day. What had she told me that we didn't already know? Annie Cormack was a biochemist setting up laboratories to make money from global warming. Nothing there, except the biochemist bit. Annie Cormack had funded Colin's research with Brightsward's money, then murdered him when he hit pay dirt. Well, we'd worked that one out, too. But what was the pay dirt? My mind stretched back to that morning in Martin's kitchen when we'd passed Colin's research diary from hand to hand, looking for clues. That's right. Global warming was going to cause the Gulf Stream to stop flowing and plunge Europe into some sort of ice age. An idea teased the corner of my mind. Elusive. Something Madeleine said at the dinner table.

I climbed out of bed and prowled softly towards the window. Leaned out and breathed the thick warm air. What was it? It was something to do with the labs. That's it. Food. Of *course*. Millions of people in their big cities. Who was going to feed them when the ice came? And they'd pay good money for food, wouldn't they? These are no Third World nations. These are the rich countries. Britain, France, Germany. No wonder Annie wanted Colin's discovery kept secret. In ten years, when Europe is plunged into a new ice age, she will be the one to supply them with food. And they will pay dearly for it, too. No worries about that.

I went back to bed and lay on my back, staring at the ceiling. Thought about the greenhouses at Quilpie. Those red squares cut out of the brown country. So what did she want with laboratories in New York and greenhouses in western Queensland? What did she plan to do? Create some sort of prototype food crop in the laboratories, then send them to be grown in the greenhouses? That sounded feasible, at least. But, no, it was madness, that's what it was. Annie

Cormack had murdered two people – three, if you counted Dr Maddern - over some crazy idea that was never going to work. Not in a million years.

I leaned down and pulled up the covers. It was past midnight and the air was a cool whisper at the window. My thoughts began rolling again. Annie wasn't mad, she couldn't be, not when she was capable of such slow, meticulous planning. First the net to catch the fish – and MMC must spread its net pretty wide, if it had found Colin in Brisbane. Then Colin's research, which must have seemed promising right from the start for her to have put plans in place to get rid of him when the time came. Not just to get rid of him, but to make sure the blame landed somewhere else. With me. Madeleine said it was a coincidence that I'd met Colin in Antarctica. But Annie wasn't in the business of coincidences. Everything happened for a reason. So why had Annie recruited me to go to Antarctica?

I remembered when I first heard she'd chosen me for the job. Middle of the wet season and I was in north Queensland ferrying supplies into Normanton while they waited for the roads to dry out. So there I was sitting in the thick atmosphere of the purple pub with a beer going rapidly warm in front of me when my mobile phone rang and Annie Cormack from Brightsward was on the other end, offering me the job of a lifetime. I remembered giving a whoop of excitement and the back-slaps of the boys when I told them the news. But even then I had wondered, why me? Why pick an inexperienced pilot who spends her time mustering cattle and crop spraying in the outback when there were all those other guys? The ones who did drilling rigs and oil fires and sea rescues. So why did she? Not because I was gay. Because I was inexperienced. How much easier to blame someone like me when the Brightsward helicopter crashed onto the ice.

But there was one thing Annie hadn't planned, couldn't plan, and that was Eric's illness. I humped over on my side and pulled the sheet over my shoulders. When did Madeleine say Eric had started getting sick? He was going to take her to Buenos Aires to see the *Astral Traveller* when the old ship returned from the Antarctic, only he was too ill to make the journey. I knew when that was. Early March. Because that was when Nicole and her hot-house lilies turned up at the hospital asking questions about the crash. It was perfect timing for Annie because, with Colin dead and his research findings tucked away deep in the bowels of MMC, she needed Eric out of the way while she bled Brightsward dry to build her laboratories.

I jerked myself upright and sat with my arms wrapped around my chest, as my heart thudded sickeningly. A coincidence? It couldn't be. Any more than anything else had been throughout this whole sorry tale. A wave of perspiration covered my body and I shivered in the cool air from the window as the thoughts whirled dizzyingly through my head. So, if it wasn't a coincidence that Eric got sick just when Annie needed him out of the way, what was going on? And then the words dropped clear into my mind and they were spoken with Martin's voice.

Poison, it's a woman's weapon.

Of course! I was on my feet, now, prowling the hot, airless room. Eric's illness was pivotal to Annie's plans and she was a poisoner. Therefore Annie must be poisoning Eric, had been for a long time. And why? Not to kill him, not this time. To keep him out of the way while she finished whatever it was she was doing in such a hurry. And then what? What was going to happen when her plans came to fruition? What was going to happen to Eric then? What was going to happen to Madeleine? Or me?

I shivered again but, this time, it was with fear. The first time I had felt real fear since I arrived in Eric's house. Martin's Arrian lay on my bedside table. I picked it up and held it to my nose, inhaling the sweet, mothbally smell of the old book that reminded me so clearly of the kitchen table at home where Martin's books and papers lay in their untidy heaps. I wished – oh, how I wished – that I was at home in Martin's shabby house by the river. In Martin's arms. But at least I could talk to him, let him know what was going through my mind. I checked my watch. Midnight. Middle of the afternoon in Australia. What was to stop me going downstairs to the office to see if Martin was on line?

My mind made up, I opened my bedroom door and stepped out. The corridor was in darkness, lit only by the yellow glow of the street lamp muffled by thick lace curtains. A white figure detached itself from the shadows and drifted towards me. The scream died in my throat as I realised it was Celeste on one of her missions into Eric's room, her arms laden with clean linen.

'You want something, madam?'

'No, I just need to use the computer.'

'Your boyfriend, heh? In Australia?'

I nodded.

'You drink your tea?'

'Yes. *Gracias.*'

'I'll take your tray.'

I pressed the button for the lift and rode it down to the ground floor, then I padded across the cool tiles in the hall and opened the office door. The office was at the front of the house and the light from the street lamp outside came through the uncurtained windows, illuminating the gloomy wood panelled walls and the impersonal office furniture. In one corner, the computer screen glowed a dull green. I bent over the keyboard and logged in. Please let Martin be on line. But then I paused, my hands poised above the keys. I couldn't just tell Martin I thought Annie was poisoning Eric, could I? I didn't know much about computers but even I could see how risky that would be. And I remembered what Madeleine had said to me out there on the fire escape. Everything is to do with Annie around here

Okay, how about this? I could use the characters from Martins's Arrian. The evil Olympias for Annie Cormack. Alexander's father, King Phillip, who may or may not have been murdered by his own son, for Eric van Eps. I grinned to myself. I had been reading Martin's book and found it curiously appealing and not at all what I'd expected. Apart from the interminable battles which, judging by the scrawl marks in the margins, were the only bits Martin was interested in, it was like reading the script for some sort of ancient history TV soap. Sex, murder and betrayal, it was all there in bucketloads.

And Martin would understand what I was doing, wouldn't he? If not, he'd just think I was turning into some sort of ancient history scholar and smile in that maddening way of his. Nothing lost, if that happened. I could try again. At least anyone listening in would be none the wiser. Hopefully.

I logged myself into Messenger and, thank God, Martin was there. I started typing.

> Zoe says:
> Hi Martin. How are you?
> Martin says:
> Good. What did you do today?
> Zoe says:
> Went to the Statue of Liberty. It was pretty good. Listen, I've been doing some research and I need to ask you something – do you think Philip is being poisoned?
> Martin says:
> Philip of Macedon? He wasn't killed by poison. What are you talking about?

Shit, I thought, he doesn't get it. How much more obvious do I have to be? Okay, try again.

> Zoe says:
> I've been doing some research of my own and I think Philip is being poisoned by someone in the palace.
> Martin says:
> Oh, okay. And who do you suspect?
> Zoe says:
> The mad queen Olympias, up to her usual tricks.
> Martin says:
> Unlikely. What would she have to gain? If he dies, Roxane will inherit his kingdom, yes?

I knew who Roxane was, had known before I started reading the book. She was Alexander's future wife, living with her father on top of the Rock of Sogdiana, in what is probably today's Afganistan, until Alexander came along and captured it. Of course, Martin was only interested in how Alexander's soldiers scaled the rock, but I'd found the story quite romantic and had imagined myself as Roxane with Martin as my very own Alexander. But now I realised Martin was using Roxane to represent Madeleine.

Zoe says:
Yes, Roxane will inherit. But I'm not talking about Philip dying.
Martin says:
What then?
Zoe says:
Just out of the way.
Martin says:
Makes sense. Do you want me to talk to Prof Wilson about it?'
Zoe says:
Yes, please. I think that's a very good idea.
Martin says:
Come home, Zoe. Leave Prof Wilson's students to sort it out.
Zoe says:
I can't. I've got Philip and Roxane to think about.
Martin says:
Okay, fair enough.
Zoe says:
Call Prof Wilson.
Martin says:
Don't worry, I'll call him now.
Zoe says:
Thanks, Martin.
Martin says:
Just take care, okay? Love you.
Zoe says:
Bye

I logged out and made my way back upstairs. The online conversation had not reassured me, but rather had made me realise how isolated I was and how far away were my friends. The breeze had turned cold now, as the short summer night headed towards dawn. I pulled the heavy sash window halfway down, then climbed into bed and pulled the sheet over me. My eyes were gritty with tiredness but I closed them resolutely and felt my heart gradually calm down as I moved towards sleep.

And then, just as I felt myself slipping away, another thought tugged me back to wakefulness. Why had Annie picked on Brightsward? It seemed an odd choice for someone out to make herself a fortune. Fair enough, she was ambitious and she'd taken her chances as they arose, but there seemed to be something almost personal about her attack on Eric and Madeleine van Eps. Almost as if she hated them.

FOURTEEN

Then it was Friday and Annie was due home that night. The day was breathless with heat. After breakfast Johannes bundled us into the car and took us for a drive through Central Park. When I had seen enough of leafy trees and lush lawns, I leaned back against the leather upholstery and closed my eyes. Looking at scenery had never been a favourite occupation of mine, unless it was from the cabin of a helicopter, and I had always found such bright green landscapes a little disturbing, as if they were not quite real. At the end of our stately circumnavigation, Johannes dropped us at the southern end of the park and we took a carriage ride which, at least, had the advantage of allowing us to enjoy what little fresh air there was on a hot August afternoon in the middle of New York.

After dinner we received our instructions from Annie, delivered by Celeste who informed us that she would not be bringing our trays upstairs that night but would serve supper in the living room after Annie's return. Despite the wide screen TV and the collection of DVDs, I was not a big fan of Eric's living room with its parquetry floor and heavy walnut furniture and that stuffy, airless smell that reminded me of my grandmother's front room at home.

My inclination was to go upstairs and lie on my bed and read my Arrian. Find out what happened to Roxane and Alexander, although I had a bad feeling there wasn't going to be a happy ending for either of them. And, to be honest, I was not sure how I would manage the meeting with Annie with what I knew about her so close to the surface of my mind. It wasn't the sort of game I was used to playing. But Madeleine was so distressed when I mentioned it that I submitted to sitting in one of Eric's scratchy arm chairs flicking the pages of the latest magazines and watching reruns on TV.

At nine o'clock we heard a car pull up outside the house, hasty footsteps on the stone steps, the slam of the front door, then Annie came into the living room, shouting for Celeste over her shoulder. She was wearing a dark blue business suit and a cream blouse, stretched tight across her breasts. She kicked off her shoes and threw herself into the arm chair opposite mine.

'Hello, girls,' she said. 'Johannes tells me you've been having fun. Ah, thank you, Celeste.' She lifted up her hands to take the tray from Celeste and settled it on her lap. 'So, tell me. What have you been doing?'

We began telling her about our sight-seeing trips while she ate her supper, the fork travelling steadily between tray and mouth as she gobbled down the food and our words in hasty bites. When she had finished she shoved the tray onto the floor and stretched out her legs.

'So what are you planning for tomorrow?'

A swift glance between us. 'We were thinking ...'

'Actually, I think you should both stay home tomorrow. It's going to be hot again and I promised Madeleine's grandfather I wouldn't let her wear herself out.' She leaned forward and tapped Madeleine playfully on the knee. 'We don't want you getting sick, do we?' she said with a look of friendly concern that didn't fit on that hard face.

Next morning after breakfast Annie called me into the office. There was a small table near the window and Annie walked round it and sat down with her back against the harsh morning light.

'Sit down,' she said, indicating the other chair. 'Nothing to worry about. It's just that Brightsward's postmaster has reported some inappropriate content in the messages you've been sending. He's the IT guy over at headquarters,' she explained in response to my puzzled look. She glanced down at a piece of paper in her hand. 'You were chatting last night to someone called Martin?'

'He's my boyfriend. In Brisbane.'

'One of your messages made reference to poison.'

'Poison's an inappropriate word?' Under the table I clasped my hands together tightly to stop them trembling.

'We believe it is. Our software is programmed to pick up words like that. And for a very good reason.' Back to the piece of paper. 'You mentioned someone called Olympias. Who's she?'

'Olympias?' I feigned a relieved look. 'She's the mother of Alexander the Great. Look, Annie, there's a simple explanation for all this. Martin's studying the history of Alexander the Great for his doctorate. He's been testing out a hypothesis about Olympias.' God, I could lie. It even sounded good to me. 'She was an ambitious woman in a world of men and she got some very bad press. He's trying to work out whether it was justified.'

'And your interest in this ... Olympias?'

I shook my head. 'I don't really have an interest in her. Martin lent me his Arrian – his history of Alexander and I've been reading it.'

'Have you got it with you?'

'It's upstairs.'

She held out her hand, like a teacher confiscating lollies. 'Can I have a look?'

'I'll go and get it.'

I went upstairs, ran cold water over my wrists to cool myself down, grabbed the Arrian and ran back down to the office. I placed my precious book into Annie's hand and waited.

She flicked through the pages, noted the heavy underlining and the scribbled notes in the margins.

'Who did all this?'

'Martin did. It's his book.'

'So what's he using now?'

'One from the library. He wanted me to have this one while I was away.' Desperation made me brave. 'Can I have it back, please?'

Annie handed me the book. 'Just take care, that's all. This is America and we all have to watch what we say. Oh, and Zoe?'

I turned back from the door. 'Yes?"

'How are you getting along with Madeleine? You seem to be having a good time together.'

'Yes, we are.'

'Good. I'm glad.' Annie stood up and walked around the table to where I was standing. 'But remember what I told you last time you were here. Don't get too close to her. Madeleine's heading for trouble and I don't want you to be a part of it.'

I went back upstairs to restore my precious book to its place on my bedside table. From Madeleine's room I could hear the sound of music, played very loud. I knocked on the connecting door but there was no reply, so I opened the door and entered Madeleine's fantasy world. At the window a breeze fluttered the purple curtains that were blocking out most of the hot morning light. In the gloomy half-light, the stars on the ceiling glowed eerily. The music pumped the air. Madeleine was sprawled on her bed among the soft toys, a newly-lit joint in her hand. The sweet smell of dope mingled sickeningly with the perfume of the half-burned candles grouped like dead things on her dressing table.

She turned her head. 'What did Annie want?'

I didn't answer her question. Instead I strode across the room, grabbed the joint from her fingers and pinched out the flame. I went to the window, flung back the curtains and tossed it out as far as I could throw. Through the red mist of my anger I saw Madeleine's startled face as she reared herself up on her elbow. But I wasn't finished yet. I went back to the bed where her long fingers were already busy stuffing the pale green weed into another cigarette paper and snatched her little tin out of her hand.

'That's enough, Madeleine,' I yelled, as my anger spilled over. 'Stop it now. Do you hear?'

Because my eyes were open. Open and taking notice. Suddenly Madeleine's drug habit was not just some bored kid smoking too much dope. I thought of Madeleine's dealer – Dimitri, was that his name? – the grocery boy who kept her so well supplied with the one thing she needed, the one thing she couldn't resist. Dimitri had a key to the kitchen, that's what Madeleine had told me. And Annie, who knew everything that happened in Eric's house, must surely know about that key. Yet she had done nothing to stop Dimitri bringing the stuff into the house, even though she hated drugs with a passion and openly despised Madeleine for her pot-smoking habit. Why? Because Eric's granddaughter was as much of a threat to Annie's plans as Eric himself, and what better way to neutralise that threat than by having her permanently stoned out of her brain? I looked down at the young girl on the bed and remembered her in the dining room the evening after we'd been to the Statue of Liberty, the spark of malice at the back of those clear, green-flecked eyes. Spilling Annie's secrets.

Oh, Annie was clever. I had to give her that. One by one she'd eliminated the people who threatened her. Colin Wilson in Antarctica. Professor McRae in Brisbane. Now she was well on her way to finishing off poor old Eric and, if she killed me too, it would be third time lucky for her and I would have no one to blame but myself. But she wasn't having Madeleine. Not if I can help it.

'Come on, Maddie,' I said in a different voice. 'Let's go and find ourselves something do.'

We spent the afternoon in the kitchen making toffee, ruining a saucepan in the process which, as I remembered too late, was an inevitable consequence of toffee making. Celeste kicked us out when it was time for her to cook dinner, a meal for which neither of us had much appetite, a result of eating so much sugar we'd nearly made ourselves sick. Still, it had been a good day.

Midnight and I needed to talk to Martin. I let myself out of my room and was aware instantly of movement in the dark corridor. Celeste again, I thought. But this time it was Annie coming from Eric's room. Annie with a small brown bottle in her hand, and an empty medicine glass smeared with a white residue. She closed Eric's door softly behind her, then took a step towards me until I could see her face clearly in the muted yellow light from the street lamp outside the window. And she could see mine. Not a word was spoken but a look of perfect understanding passed between us. A confirmation, if either of us needed one, of what the other was up to.

Then, 'Is everything okay, Zoe?'

'I ... I'm just going down to the kitchen. I need a drink.'

'You've had your tea, haven't you?'

'Yes, but I want a cold drink. It's so hot tonight.'

Annie nodded. 'Well, go quietly. Eric doesn't like people wandering around at night. It disturbs his rest.'

She tried to make me feel like a child but, this time, it didn't work. Because now I knew who she was and all I felt was hate. And a creeping, ugly fear.

I went down to the kitchen and got myself a can of soft drink from the big refrigerator. Sat at the table while I drank it. Outside in the little yard Celeste's herbs bled their fragrance into the humid air. Then I went back upstairs through the silent, listening house. Because how could I use the computer now? How could I talk to Martin when I knew Anne was going to read, and interpret, every word I wrote?

In my room I sat by the window, staring at the banked clouds above the opposite building, stained a lurid yellow by the lights of the city. I was shivering. Because suddenly I realised what Annie had been telling me outside in the corridor. Not just that she was poisoning Eric. She didn't care if I knew that. She was telling me that she could do what she liked. To Eric, to Madeleine, to everyone in the house. And, when it was my turn, she'd do what she liked to me.

FIFTEEN

The next morning Annie decided to let us out. Johannes brought the car round to the front of the house and we dutifully climbed inside. He drove out of the city to Cape Cod where the rich people's houses squatted among the dunes and there was a long sand bar and then the ocean, grey and sullen under the threatening sky. It was going to rain later, Madeleine said so and I believed her. It couldn't help it after so many stifling days. Walking down to the beach I could feel the city's hot breath on the back of my neck.

Johannes took a picnic basket out of the boot, dumped it on the sand and retreated to the car. Madeleine and I sat miserably on the gritty sand, huddled in beach towels, watching an expensive dog barking at sea gulls. Once again I felt the home-hunger deep in my soul. But not for Martin this time. Today I was thinking of hot white sand and warm blue water and mangroves fringing a muddy, fish-filled creek. What was wrong with these people that they could think there was anything beautiful about this place?

Beside me, Madeleine was doing a good impression of a sulky kid, not so keen today on the restriction I had imposed on her. But we sat it out as long as we could while the storm clouds gathered on the horizon and the air trembled with distant thunder. Because, at the end of the day, we had to go back to that house. And Annie Cormack.

I arrived home with a headache, the kind I used to get in Bowen when the low pressure systems swung in from the ocean and brewed up bad weather over the hills. I lay on my bed and tried to sleep. I woke to a familiar smell and to the responsibility I'd laid upon myself. To keep Madeleine off the weed. With a sigh I climbed off my crumpled bed and went to find something to keep her busy. That night we ate dinner in the kitchen because Annie had gone out. The window was wide open, fluttering Celeste's white lace curtains and letting in the stale, traffic-tainted air.

After dinner I returned to my room while Madeleine went to say good night to her grandfather. I leaned my elbows on the window sill and stared out at what I could see of the sky. I was unaware Madeleine had come into the room until I felt her arms around my waist. She leaned her head on my shoulder. 'What are you listening for?'

I turned my head. 'Thunder. Surely it will rain soon.'

'It's raining now.'

Outside the raining was falling so lightly I hadn't noticed. But now I could see it drifting past the lights from the house opposite and then, suddenly heavier, hissing on the metal of the fire escape. The cool breeze was like a sigh of relief.

'Smell it, Zoe. There'll be a storm later.'

She was still leaning against me and I could feel her skinny body pressed up against mine. 'I know what you're doing for me,' she said. 'And I'm grateful. But it isn't easy.'

'It won't be for much longer. I'm getting you out of here. You and Eric.'

A long breath, like a sigh. 'When?'

'As soon as I can. Look, Maddie. I need to use the computer. Will you come with me?'

'Sure.'

It was nine o'clock and the house was quiet. We met nobody in the corridor, or in the hall downstairs. But still we talked in whispers as we creaked open the office door and flicked on the light. The computer was switched on and it came to life when I moved the mouse. I logged on to Messenger and stared disbelieving at my list of contacts. Martin was off line. Not busy, not away. Off line. Even so, I flicked up a dialogue box and started to type.

> Zoe says:
> Martin, will you please contact Prof Wilson ASAP and ask him to talk to his colleagues in New York. I think I need their help

I hit OK and closed down the window. There, it was done. Once Annie read my message she would act against me. Nothing was surer. But maybe, just maybe, help would arrive in time. In the meantime, all I had to do was keep calm and act normal. Whatever normal was supposed to be.

I turned my head and looked up at Madeleine. 'Is there anything you want to do while we're down here?' I said, more cheerfully than I was feeling.

'What about looking up that institute you were talking about the other day?'

'The MMC?'

'Yeah. If it's a legitimate organisation, it should have a web site.'

'Okay, then. You go.'

I stood up and let Madeleine take the chair in front of the screen. She clicked onto Firefox, and typed in MMC then hit Search. The result was a bland web page containing little more than a banner headline and a menu down the left hand side.

Madeleine leaned forward. 'What do you want to look at?'

'Try that one.' I pointed over her shoulder. 'Our research.'

A click took us to another page. According to the blurb, the MMC Research Institute was a benevolent organisation dedicated to finding answers to the world's most pressing environmental problems, most of which were listed. There were live links to the usual suspects. I pointed again.

'Here you go. Global warming.'

Another click and I was looking at Colin's face. Colin's face without a bullet hole in the forehead. Colin's face as I remembered it on Midsummer Eve. Friendly, intelligent eyes. A wry smile creasing his mouth. Seriously attractive. There was a report on his research. It was as bland as everything else on the site.

'Go back,' I said. 'See if there's anything about food. Remember the other night? You said it was one of the things Annie's labs were working on.'

Madeleine clicked back to the home page and we stared at the list.

'So what have we got? Green power. Desalination. Carbon

sinks. Food technology.' I pointed. There you go. Try that one'

Madeleine opened the page then stood up. 'You read it. You know what you're looking for.'

I slipped into the chair in front of the screen. 'Okay, usual stuff. Malthus and his doom and gloom theory.'

'Wasn't he the guy who said we'd die of starvation when the food supply ran out?'

'That's him. We were all supposed to be dead about 150 years ago.' I turned back to the screen. 'Blah blah, blah … Green Revolution … Well, we know about that, don't we? New strains of wheat and rice saved the Third World from starvation in the Fifties? Sixties?'

'Sixties, I think it was.'

'Okay, here we go. Listen to this. *Thanks to nanotechnology, tomorrow's food will be designed by shaping molecules and atoms. In agriculture, nanotechnology promises to reduce pesticide use, and improve plant and animal breeding. It's estimated that in ten years' time the nanofood market will be worth $20.4 billion.* So that's what she's up to. Designer food. Create it in the laboratory, grow it in the greenhouses. And a market of millions just around the corner.'

I turned my head but Madeleine had stopped listening. She'd left the desk and was prowling restlessly around the room.

'See that door?' She pointed at the dark-panelled wall on the far side of the room. 'You know what's through there? Annie's bedroom. Do you want to take a look?' A strange, eager, expression. Dangerous. 'I've always wondered what it was like in her room.'

I felt a quick flicker of excitement. Curiosity. And anger, too. Seeing Colin's image has released a surge of anger, like a drug. Not a good emotion to replace caution, the one thing Mr Wilson had told me to hang onto, the only thing that was going to get us out alive.

Some caution remained. 'What if she comes back?'

Madeleine shook her head. 'She won't. It's Sunday night. She'll stay out drinking with her pals.'

'Okay then.'

It was like a nun's cell. Bare wooden floor. White walls. A narrow bed pushed against the far wall. Next to the bed a table piled with books. No window. The silence was claustrophobic.

'I don't know how she stands it,' I said.

But Madeleine didn't reply. I turned around. She was staring at a photograph in a heavy wooden frame hanging on the wall above Annie's bed. An old woman. Iron grey hair. Lantern jaw. Piercing eyes that would have been blue except the photograph was in black and white.

'Who is she?'

Madeleine turned her head. 'I don't know who she is. But I know that face. I've seen her somewhere before. I know I have.'

But I had no time to reply. There was the sound of a taxi door slamming outside in the street, hurried feet on the stone steps, the scrape of a key in the lock. Annie came into the hall, wiping her feet on the mat and shouting cheerfully for Celeste. There was a moment's horrified silence. Through the open door of Annie's bedroom I could see the trail we'd left behind us. Lights on in the office. The computer screen showing MMC's web page. The connecting door wide open.

I turned to Madeleine. 'What do we do?'

'I'll show you. Come on!'

She flicked around and ran for the corner of the room. Another door, hidden in the panelling. Inside, a stairwell with narrow stone steps spiralling upwards. I followed Madeleine's hurrying feet and slammed the door shut behind me. Another door, but Madeleine shook her head.

'No, that's Opa's room. We have to go higher. Come on!'

The next door was solid metal, painted grey. Madeleine pushed it open and we were on the roof in the pouring rain. Through the grey murk I saw the small black beetle shape of the helicopter crouched on its painted circle.

I paused for a moment to suck in a lungful of the cool, sweet air. But Madeleine was running across the bitumen surface of the roof. She slung one leg over the low brick parapet and disappeared. With my heart beating loudly in my throat, I followed her and saw her slight figure disappearing down the fire escape which clung like spindly black scaffolding to the back of the house.

I swallowed my fear and climbed over the wall. By the time I reached the landing outside our bedrooms, she was inside her room, panting and laughing.

'I haven't done that for a long time,' she said, and fell backwards onto the bed, still laughing.

'Do you think we got away with it?' I put my hand on my chest to stop the hammering of my heart.

'No, she knows. But what can she do?'

I sat down on the edge of the bed. 'Madeleine, that photograph. Who is she?'

Madeleine sat up. 'I don't know.' She turned her head and stared at me. 'But, if it's someone I recognise, what's it doing hanging in Annie's bedroom?'

A tap at the door. Celeste came in carrying Madeleine's tray.

'Your tea is in your room, Miss Zoe,' she said to me. 'Best go to bed now, I think?'

'Thanks, Celeste.' I stood up and scraped my fingers through my wet hair. 'I think I'll go and have a shower,' I said to Madeleine. 'See you in the morning.'

After my shower, I sat in the chair by the window listening to the hiss of rain on the fire escape. I poured my tea and held the cup in my hands, breathing in its warm fragrance. I took a sip and was instantly aware of a bitter taste at the back of my throat that took me back to the American doctor in Antarctica and the drug he'd slipped into my arm.

I spat out what I had in my mouth and ran to the bathroom. I turned on the tap and thrust my head under the water, swallowing great gulps. But it was too late. As the drug gripped my brain, I thought back to my darling Martin, leaning against the kitchen bench at home while the kettle steamed gently behind him.

Poison. It's a woman's weapon.

So finally Annie Cormack, the do-it-yourself biochemist with her bagful of dirty tricks had done to me what she'd done to all the rest. And I had let her do it.

SIXTEEN

I woke to find myself lying on Madeleine's bed. My arms were above my head, tied to the bed head with the sheer purple curtains that used to hang from the bed's canopy. My brain was thumping so hard it felt like it was about to jump out of my head. The air in the room was hot and still, smelling of the scented candles on Madeleine's dressing table. Outside, thunder growled. I turned my head and there was Madeleine lying next to me, her face as white as a sheet. Already my shoulders ached. Annie finished the final knot with a vicious tug and stepped away from the bed to survey her handiwork.

'You recognised her, didn't you? In that photograph in my bedroom?' She spoke to Madeleine across my body. 'That's Maggie Mary. Your grandmother and mine.' She took a step closer to the bed. 'I'm your sister, you silly little bitch. Or hadn't you figured that one out yet? You and your nosy pal.' A grin of triumph. 'It doesn't matter anyway. Not any more. Because now I'm going to kill you both.'

'You're not my sister.'

'Yes I am. We have the same father, you and me. We grew up in the same shitty apartment in New Jersey. Maggie Mary raised you from a baby while your mom was busy shooting up anything she could lay her hands on.' Annie prowled across the room and picked up one of Madeleine's candles. The smell of jasmine drifted in the humid air. 'And you know what? I was glad when your mom died because it made us even. I didn't have to hate you quite so much.'

There was a crack of thunder, followed by a deep booming rumble that rolled away into the distance. Annie came back to the bed and stared down at Madeleine. 'But then your grandfather turned up in a big car and took you away. Maggie Mary said you were going to live in a fancy house and we should be happy because a bit of good might come our way. But – you know what? - it never did. How do you think that made me feel, huh?'

'Where is your father – our father – now?'

Annie shrugged. 'Dead or in prison. Why should I care? He was a drug dealer. That's why I hate them – dealers and drugs alike. That's what killed my mom.'

'Your mom and mine,' said Madeleine quietly. 'We're the same, you and me.'

Annie lifted her lip in a sneer. 'We're not the same. Look at you. What have you ever done except have a rich grand-daddy?'

I turned my head. 'And what have you done? Lied and cheated. Killed everyone that got in your way. I suppose that's something to be proud of?'

'I look after myself,' she snarled.

'So how many more deaths before you get what you want? It must be worth it for you to go to so much trouble.'

'Oh, yes, it's worth it all right. And I'm nearly through. By morning you and my sister will be dead from an overdose. The press will have a field day for a day or two, until something new comes along. Because who in New York is going to mourn another drug-addled heiress found in the gutter? Then it will be Eric's turn. The poor guy's been on death's door for a week. It's about time I put him out of his misery.' She came around the bed and thrust her face into mine. I could smell garlic on her breath. 'Killing *you* will be my pleasure. You've been a thorn in my side ever since you got back from the Antarctic. And, if the person I trusted to do the job hadn't ballsed it up, you never would have gotten back in the first place, You'd have been snap-frozen down the nearest crevasse like your little mate.'

'Who …?'

'Work it out for yourself,' sneered Annie. 'You've worked out everything else. You and your pals in Brisbane.'

I shut my eyes while the nightmare spooled through my

brain. The skidoo, black against the shimmering snow. A rifle pointing towards my helicopter. I remembered the sweat coursing over my body as I fought to control my craft.

I stared up at my tormentor. 'I don't know who it was. Why don't you tell me?'

'So she finally doesn't know something.' Annie grinned nastily. 'There's only one person it could be. Did you know Nicole was a crack shot? Won medals for it. Pity she couldn't manage the one job I asked her to do. One shot, I told her. One shot through the rotors and she'd be done. Mission accomplished. She got rid of *him* on the ice. A nice neat shot through the head. But you …' Annie shrugged. 'That hole in your leg was an extra. She did what she could. Bashed your leg to hide the bullet wound, then left you to die on the ice. It was just her bad luck the Amundsen guys heard your 'copter come down. And there wasn't much she could do when they contacted her to come and take you away except thank them nicely and cart you back to the ship.'

'The bullet?'

'Came out in Argentina. And we would have gotten away with it, too, only you found the only doctor in Bowen who knew what he was looking at.'

'He's dead now. For a while I thought you'd killed him.'

'I would have done, only your brother-in-law beat me to it.'

'There's one thing I can't understand.' I stared up at her. 'You've wanted me dead ever since the helicopter accident. So why didn't you kill me the last time I was here?'

'Because I was … persuaded that you weren't a threat. Too busy shagging that new boy friend of yours. But you weren't just shagging him, were you? You were poking your nose where it didn't belong. The pair of you.'

I narrowed my eyes and felt pain pierce my brain like a hot needle. An echo reverberated somewhere among the aching jumble of my thoughts. Someone else had used those words. I struggled to grasp the memory. That's it. My sister. *What are you playing at, Zoe?* I remembered the good wine and the bright glare of the new TV. And I knew what Annie was going to say before she said it.

'So how is Zara these days? I haven't spoken with her in quite a while. She's a very helpful girl, your sister. There isn't anything in the world she wouldn't do. For money.'

I shut my eyes wearily and thought about Annie leaving the whale stranding the morning after I told her about my leg. Up north to Bowen. To get rid of Dr Maddern, only my brother-in-law beat her to it. And to recruit my sister as a spy. No wonder she'd been so keen to invite me back to New York the second time around. She knew what I'd been up to in the mean time.

I stared up into Annie's face. 'Okay, you win. So why don't you get on with it? Then I won't have to keep looking at your ugly face.'

Annie lifted her arm and I braced for her hard hand to smash into my face. But then she grinned and shrugged.

'See you soon, girls,' she said, then turned and walked towards the door, still holding the jasmine-scented candle. A flick of the light switch plunged the room into black, storm-filled darkness. I turned my head and there was Madeleine's head on the other pillow, her eyes like black bruises in her pale, milk-white face.

'What's going on, Zoe? What's happening?'

'Annie's going to kill us.'

'But why? I don't understand.'

'To get what she wants. I thought it was greed, but it's revenge, too. I didn't know she was your sister.'

It was the last piece of the puzzle. The piece that answered the question I had been asking ever since my helicopter crashed into the ice. *Why?* Not to make money, although that was part of it. To have her revenge. On Eric, for rescuing his grand daughter. On Madeleine, for being rescued. Annie blamed them both for the misery she had endured year after year during her childhood, and her hatred towards them had grown like a cancer in her soul.

'If it's any comfort,' I said, 'my sister isn't much better.'

We were silent for a while. Outside, muffled by the heavy glass in the window, the storm continued to rage. It was raining heavily now. I moved my arms, trying to keep the blood flowing into my fingers. Already my body was a shriek of pain that reminded me of the day the Americans took out the drips and handed me over to Brightsward. The drug was pounding in my brain, drowning thought.

Then Madeleine said, 'Maggie Mary Cormack, Zoe. Annie named the institute after her grandmother.'

'The MMC Research Institute,' I said, remembering Mr Wilson outside the coffee shop handing over the florist's card. That good old cop had warned me not to go snooping around but I'd ignored him. Story of my life, really. Zoe knows best. Well, not this time.

'Do you remember her?'

'I don't remember much,' said Madeleine's voice in the darkness. 'Just that face and the sound of her voice. I used to run to my bed and hide when she started yelling. There was another girl in the bed with me who used to comfort me when I cried. I guess it must have been Annie. Funny how things turn out.'

Oh, yes, hilarious, I thought. Remembering how Zara and I used to huddle sweating under the covers while Bowen's violent thunderstorms raged through the night. Sisterhood. It was the most poisonous relationship known to mankind, especially when money was involved. Madeleine and I were the living proof of that. Here we lay side by side in the stuffy heat of Madeleine's bedroom where our sisters had put us. Waiting to die.

I turned my head on the pillow. 'We haven't had much luck, have we?'

Madeleine smiled at me. 'I have. I met you.'

'You mean that?'

'Sure I do.'

I felt something seize my heart and squeeze it in an agony of joy. Tears began flowing from my eyes, hot and stinging. I made no attempt to stop them.

'Look, Madeleine, I'm going to say something to you and I don't want you to take it the wrong way. I love you, okay? If I could pick my sister I'd choose you. I wish this wasn't happening, I really do. Because I'm just getting to know you and I'd like some more time.'

'Don't cry, Zoe.'

'You know what else? I never told Martin I loved him. And now it's too late.'

'He knows.'

'Maybe he does. But I didn't say it. I wish I had. If I had one wish before I die, that would be it.' And then, 'What was that?'

Madeleine turned her head. 'What?'

'I thought I heard something.'

Silence while we strained our ears.

'There it is again,' I said. 'It sounds like windows smashing. What's going on?'

'I … I dunno. Zoe … can you smell smoke?'

'Smoke?' Then I could smell it, too. 'Where's it coming from? It's pouring with rain outside.'

The smell of smoke grew stronger. Downstairs windows were breaking in a regular rhythm. Crash! Crash! Crash! And then there was a loud knocking on the window of our room.

'Madeleine? You in there?'

'It's Dimitri,' said Madeleine. 'Dimitri!' she yelled. 'Quick! Break the window.'

The knocking grew louder. Then the window smashed in a shower of broken shards. The sound of the rain pounding on the fire escape invaded our quiet space. The smell of smoke was stronger now and I could see a flickering orange glow somewhere below the window.

Dimitri was young, dark-haired, painfully thin. He was possessed of an edgy energy that brought him quickly to the side of the bed.

'Madeleine, what the fuck's goin' on?'

'Never mind what's going on,' said Madeleine. 'Just get us untied. Quickly.'

'Is the house on fire?' I asked.

'The kitchen is.' Dimitri bent down and began picking at the knots that tied Madeleine's hands.

'So what happened?'

'That bitch Annie was down in the kitchen, right? And she had a candle burning. Some kinda yellow candle. And it smelled like … I dunno what the fuck it smelled like. Some kinda fucken flower. *Fuck* ...' He pulled his hand away from the knot and shook it. 'Fuck, that hurt.'

'Dimitri,' said Madeleine. 'Scissors. In the drawer.'

Dimitri crossed the floor and pulled open the top drawer of Madeleine's dressing table. He turned his head.

'In here?'

'Yeah, they're my panties.' Madeleine was almost crying with frustration. '*Underneath*, Dimitri! Don't pretend you've never seen them before.'

Dimitri plunged his hand into the drawer and came up with the little silver scissors Madeleine used for chopping up. He came back to the bed and began hacking at the purple curtains around Madeleine's wrists.

'Annie called me about an hour ago and asked for some junk. I thought it was kinda strange because I know how much she hates the stuff. But she had all the gear laid out on the table cloth – the spoon, the belt, the syringe. And she's going, give it to me, give it to me. And I've brought enough skag to kill a donkey stone dead. There you go ...'

Madeleine's first hand was free. She lowered her arm and shook it vigorously.

Dimitri began on the second hand, sawing away with frantic haste. '... and she's acting kinda weird. I mean she's always been a crazy bitch but this is different. It's her eyes or sump'n, I dunno. And I think, she's gonna kill someone with this stuff. So I say no, no, and she kinda lunges at me and tries to grab the stuff outta my hand.'

The scissors cut through the last of the purple curtain and Madeleine jerked upright, rubbing her wrists.

'Give me the scissors.'

She limped around the bed and began hacking at the curtain holding my arms to the bed. 'Oh, shit, oh fuck,' she muttered. 'Sorry, Zoe, pins and needles. So then what, Dimitri?'

'So then we were fighting in the middle of the kitchen. Annie's a big, tough bitch and she's hitting me around the head. I thought she was gonna fucken kill me. But then I kinda pushed her and she fell against the table. The candle tipped over and the flame just went whoosh across the cloth and up those frilly curtains your house maid … what's her name?'

'… Celeste …'

'Yeah, Celeste. She put them up at the window to make herself feel at home. And the flames just climbed up 'em.'

'Then what happened? There you go, Zoe.'

I sat up slowly, feeling the blood flowing sluggishly down my arms.

He lifted his narrow shoulders. 'I came straight up here to make sure you were all right.'

'So what happened to Annie?'

'I dunno,' said Dimitri. 'Fuck her, Madeleine. Let's get out of here.'

Madeleine shook her head. 'No, I've got to rescue Opa – my grandfather. You go …'

'What about her?' Dimitri flicked his finger in my direction.

I was sitting on the side of the bed feeling sick and dizzy. 'I'll be okay.'

'She doesn't look okay.'

'I'll be fine.' I jerked up my head and watched the room dip and sway. 'Look, Madeleine, if we can get Eric up the stairs to the roof I can fly us out of here. The roof's closer and it'll be safer than going down towards the fire.'

'Come on, then.' Madeleine came over to the bed and grasped my elbow. She turned her head. 'Thanks, Dimitri. You okay to get out?'

Dimitri already had one skinny leg slung over the window sill. He turned and grinned. 'See you around, huh?'

But Madeleine had turned away. She had her arm across my back and was half-dragging, half-carrying me towards her bedroom door. In the corridor the smell of smoke was overpowering. I felt the adrenalin hit my body and pushed myself away.

'Come on.'

We burst through the door into Eric's bedroom. He was sitting on the edge of the bed. His appearance was shocking. Grey hair, grey skin, his body skeletal, his movements slow and halting. Next to him loomed Johannes. He was bent over Eric like a mother over her baby. He had a checked woollen dressing gown in his hand and had managed to get one of Eric's arms into a sleeve. He turned his head as we came into the room.

'Miss Madeleine? Miss Zoe? What are you doing here?'

He dropped the dressing gown on the bed and strode towards us. I had never managed to work out whose side Johannes was on. Now I was going to find out.

SEVENTEEN

Madeleine grabbed Johannes' arm. 'You've got to help us, Johannes. We need to get Opa to the roof. Zoe is gonna fly him out.'

Johannes swivelled his eyes towards me. 'You can do it?'

'Yes! I flew the Brightsward helicopter in Antarctica.'

'A good idea, then. You will need the key.' He reached into his trouser pocket and pulled out a bunch of keys. He detached one and handed it to me.

Madeleine had gone to the side of the bed and was crouched in front of her grandfather. 'Opa? Opa!'

'Huh?' It was like he was half- asleep.

'Come on, Opa. We've got to get you out.'

There was a loud crash outside the bedroom door. Orange flames burst from the lift well. The heat reached out greedily across the width of the corridor. I slammed the door shut.

'It's the only way now.'

One on each side, Johannes and Madeleine got their arms under Eric's shoulders and heaved him to his feet.

'The door, Zoe.'

Madeleine indicated the dark-panelled door opposite the window. I pulled it open and thick grey smoke rolled into the room. I took the stairs as fast as I could and emerged on the flat roof of the house. The storm had passed over now, leaving behind the cold, pelting rain and the steady, menacing roar of the fire below my feet. Behind me I was aware of Johannes and Madeleine coming out of the door with Eric slumped between them. I put my head down and ran through the rain, ignoring the screams of protest from my battered body. Up into the cockpit and push the key into the ignition. Flick the switch and set the rotors in motion. Watch as Johannes wrenches open the passenger door.

'You first,' he says to Madeleine. 'You'll have to hold him.'

He holds Eric in his arms while Madeleine clambers into the passenger seat, then passes him up to her like a giant, lifeless puppet.

'What about you?' yells Madeleine over the roar of the rotors.

Johannes shakes his head. 'No room for me. You go.' He slams the door shut and whacks the side of the helicopter. Go! Go!

And then, with surprising agility for so big a man, he runs across the bitumen, hooks a neatly trousered leg over the parapet and disappears from view.

I twist the throttle and feel the helicopter lift from the roof. I make some height and fly out over the street. The house is a column of flames. Down below I can see Dimitri with his arm around Celeste's shoulders. Johannes, looking up and punching the air with his fist. And somebody else. Martin. Stepping out of a cab that has somehow managed to nose its way through the jam of emergency vehicles blocking the street. He stands on the sidewalk in the pouring rain staring up at the wall of flames. I see Johannes touch his arm and point upwards. Martin's dearly familiar face tips up and then he lifts his arm and waves, a slow, laconic Aussie wave like he's brushing flies away from his face. And I feel my heart soar with joy.

'I love you, Martin,' I breathe as I lift the helicopter into the night sky.

I land the helicopter in Central Park, climb out stiffly and stand in the rain waiting for Martin to find me. Police cars arrive, sirens blaring, and Eric is helped out of the helicopter and into a waiting ambulance. Johannes arrives at a run and drapes his jacket over Madeleine's shoulders before scrambling into the back of the ambulance, just as the doors are closing. Then, finally, Martin is there gazing wildly around the chaotic scene. I yell his name and step forward. Into his arms.

Much later that night we found ourselves in a hotel room, sitting side by side on a plush sofa in a room that was as big as the whole of Martin's house in Brisbane. Martin was devouring a hamburger that would have stopped anyone except an impoverished student dead in his tracks. Devouring it one-handed because I was holding onto his other hand with both of mine. And I wasn't letting go.

'So what happened?' I asked. 'I only sent you that message last night. And you were off line.'

'That's because I was already on my way over here.' He gulped down the last of his hamburger and wiped his mouth with a paper napkin. 'It was your first message that did it. The one about Olympias poisoning Philip. That was a clever idea, by the way, using them as a code for Annie and Eric.'

'I don't think it fooled Annie.'

'That's what I was afraid of. As soon as you'd logged off I rang Mr Wilson and he got in touch with the counter-terrorism boys and told them everything.' Martin leaned back. 'I was all for sending in the troops straight away but Mr Wilson preferred a softly, softly approach. He said the situation was poised on a knife edge and he didn't want anything to happen that might push Annie over. And he reckoned the cops turning up at the front door would be just the thing to do it. So he made them promise to hold off for forty eight hours to give me time to get over here and get you out. Then he drove me to the airport and shoved me on a plane.' He shook his head. 'I don't know how he did it.'

'He was right about the knife edge.' I said. 'But I didn't need the cops to tip Annie over. I did that all by myself.'

'How?'

'By snooping around. The one thing Mr Wilson told me not to do.'

'Oh, Zoe.' Martin turned to face me and put his spare hand softly on my cheek. 'If you could have hung on. Just that little bit longer.'

'It worked out okay. Madeleine's drug dealer got us out.'

'I don't think it was okay. You nearly died.' He reached for me and held me tight. 'I love you, Zoe. I don't know what I'd do without you.'

I leaned my face into the warmth of his body. 'I love you, too,' I said and wondered why I'd found it so hard to say before.

Brightsward's founder moves his headquarters to Australia

Following a fire at his New York home that nearly cost him his life, environmentalist Eric van Eps has moved to Australia where he has established an experimental farm outside Quilpie in Queensland's west.

Mr van Eps recently announced a change in Brightsward's direction from its role as environmental watchdog to a more active role solving some of the world's most pressing problems.

'There's much work to be done and I am looking forward to the challenge,' said Mr van Eps, seen here with his granddaughter on their property in outback Queensland.

After the interview, I'd taken the photographer for a spin in my brand new helicopter so he could take pictures of those amazing greenhouses from the air. We'd invited the news crew to a barbeque lunch but, once the photographer was back on solid ground, they were anxious to be off on the long journey back to civilization. Now I was sitting on the veranda watching the sunlight winking off the greenhouses in the distance while Johannes set the long table in the shade of the poinciana tree. Dressed in long khaki shorts and a white shirt, he looked as if he needed a pith helmet and a shot gun to complete the picture, instead of a striped apron and a basket of cutlery.

It was midsummer, almost a year since Colin's death, and, despite the drought, the poinciana was coming into bloom. By Christmas it would be a mass of scarlet flowers. The months since the fire had been taken up with Eric's long recovery in hospital followed by a flurry of activity once he'd made up his mind that he and Madeleine were moving to Australia.

One of my first trips after my return to Queensland had been to Quilpie where I'd spent a pleasurable half hour sacking Annie's manager, the man who had threatened me with a rifle when I'd flown over the farmstead with Martin's

155

father. Then I'd taken over the homestead and, by the time Eric was ready to travel, it was clean and comfortable though, to judge from Johannes' appalled reaction, you'd think I was asking Eric to sleep in the barn. Which would have been an impossibility in any case because that's where I kept my helicopter. It took me a while to get used to the idea that my new baby was a piece of working equipment and I think I would have wrapped it in a quilt, if I'd been able to find one big enough.

Now I thought back to the first night we'd spent in the house. Back then, Johannes was still defying Queensland's early summer heat and he was dressed formally in a dark dinner suit as he waited on a table set with the sad contents of the china cupboard in the kitchen. It had been a festive occasion. Eric sat at the head of the table, tired from the journey but in high spirits. Though his hair was permanently white, he had regained a healthy colour and had put some weight back onto his bones. And his enthusiasm had returned, shining from his eyes and energising everyone he met. This was the Eric I remembered from the Brightsward promos back in the days of my recruitment and I was overjoyed to find his spirit was unquenched by his ill-health and the near-tragedy of the fire.

Madeleine, too, was filled with an irrepressible happiness. She had taken to outback life as if born to it, gained a sweet honey tint to her skin and a confident way of walking that had all the young men in town twisting their heads to watch her go by. 'Just like a deodorant ad,' I'd said sourly, the first time I saw it happen. But she'd just laughed, a delicious gurgle I'd never heard before. 'You've got Martin. Why should you care if all the boys look at me?'

As I sat under the slow-turning fan watching Johannes tackle the enormous leg of lamb that had been a house-warming gift from Martin's father, I thought back to my first dinner with the van Eps in New York. Eric sick. Madeleine subdued. And those two murderous women – Annie and Nicole – sitting across the table with their nasty little secrets hidden behind their complacent smiles.

The firemen had found Annie's body and the drug paraphernalia in the burned out kitchen of Eric's house and the press had given her the label she'd planned for us. It was a sweet revenge except that there was no undoing the harm she'd done to her victims. Of Nicole there was no sign. Like the rat she was, she'd disappeared down a drain pipe and the best efforts of New York's police could not find out where she'd gone.

After we'd eaten, Eric called Johannes to the table. He was in the kitchen stacking the dishwasher and was reluctant to come into the dining room and sit at the table with us. Eric had already absorbed the democratic nature of outback life but was having problems making Johannes see things his way. When he was seated and had a beer in front of him, Eric started to speak.

'Well, here we are at last. A new life starting. And it is Zoe we have to thank.' He raised his glass of mineral water in my direction. 'It is because of her we are here. Otherwise we would be ...' He shook his head. 'I don't want to think about where we would be. It was a bad time and it is over. But I need to talk about Annie Cormack one last time'. His face twisted in a spasm and he took a gulp of water. 'She was an evil woman but she laid the groundwork for what we are going to achieve right here in Queensland.'

Eric put his big hands flat on the table in front of him and stared around at us all. The pause had been perfected during his long years in business and he used it to good effect.

'Food production, my friends. If Zoe's friend was correct and this big freeze happens in Europe they will need someone to make food for them. It could be Brightsward doing that.' He downed the rest of his drink and slumped back in his chair. 'Whatever happens, there are people in the world right now who don't have enough to eat. We will work hard to make this nanotechnology work and who knows? We could start a new food revolution and nobody in the world will ever be hungry again.' He looked down at his empty glass, then up at Johannes. 'Damn it, Johannes, go and open a bottle of champagne. I don't care what the doctors say.'

When the champagne was open and poured into our glasses, Eric raised his in a toast. 'To Zoe Carter. The best damned helicopter pilot in the world.'

I smiled now at the memory of that night. The first bottle of champagne had disappeared, evaporated in the heat, Eric said, and Johannes had fetched another. We'd taken the second bottle out onto the verandah and sat in companionable silence watching a huge yellow moon swimming in the warm sky. I'd turned to Madeleine.

'I wonder if you'll be able to smell the storms out here?'

She'd smiled back. 'I won't have to smell them. I'll be able to see them coming.' And she'd stretched her arms above her head. 'I still can't get used to the silence.'

Which was strange from someone who'd complained long and loud about the possums on the roof waking her up at night.

Now Madeleine came out into the sunshine carrying two glasses of wine. She handed one to me and sat down on the chair next to mine.

'Back to Brisbane tomorrow?'

I sipped the cold wine. 'Yeah, I reckon. I don't want to leave Martin by himself for too long. He needs me to make sure he eats properly and goes to bed once in a while. Not that kind of bed, Madeleine,' I laughed. The girl was impossibly romantic. 'Or, at least, not every night.'

Martin and I had flown back to Australia a couple of days after the fire. As we'd crossed the date line, flying high in the freezing stratosphere, Martin had asked me to marry him. I hadn't given him an answer. It wasn't really the time or the place for making what could be the most important decision of my life.

Sure, we had champagne and dim lights – we were supposed to be sleeping – but it was awkward holding hands across the wide space that separated our Business Class seats, and a celebratory fuck was totally out of the question. Not just because I didn't fancy a shag in an aircraft toilet, but I was spaced out with travelling and all I really wanted to do was get home so I could lay my head on a cool pillow and go to sleep.

I still wasn't sure if I was going to say yes. I didn't know much about marriage and what I did know wasn't all that encouraging. And my relationship with Martin was too important to stuff up with something that might be no better than what we already had. I hadn't spoken to Zara since I got back to Australia but I knew my brother-in-law had spun enough shit to avoid a jail sentence and had moved back in with my sister. Now I knew what Zara was capable of, I was not sure which of them to pity the most.

I turned my head and smiled at Madeleine. She was my sister now, chosen on the night we'd lain together on her bed staring up at the luminous stars on the ceiling, the night we'd almost died at the hands of her own half-sister, Annie Cormack. Madeleine was desperate for me to get married so she could be my bridesmaid and I think she had the whole thing planned already, right down to how to fasten the Just Married sign to the back of my 'copter. So I'd have to see how I felt when Martin finally finished writing his thesis.

In the meantime I had plenty to keep me happy. Not just flying the helicopter which was my own personal dream come true, but there was a new expedition to plan. Eric had learned a valuable lesson from Annie, that it wasn't enough for Brightsward to publicise the world's environmental problems, it had to start solving them, too. He had expressed an interest in sending researchers to areas in the tropics currently suffering environmental damage – coral bleaching on the Great Barrier Reef, deforestation in New Guinea, mud slides in the Philippines. The planning he had handed over to Madeleine and to me. Our first job was to find the researchers we needed and it was an odd experience to return to the university where I'd first met Martin and be welcomed with open arms by scientists eager for Brightsward's cash. And I must say, once you got off ground level and into their fancy boardrooms, the coffee tasted a whole lot better.

Now I leaned back and sipped my wine, sniffing the alluring aroma of meat cooking on a wood fire. Life was good. And it was only going to get better.